For example, his little sister Piper. Nico couldn't control anything about her constantly borrowing his best hoodie, barging into his room asking to play at the most inconvenient times, or singing loudly during the long car ride to gymnastics. He also couldn't control things like the school cafeteria serving fish sticks on Mondays, the amount of homework he got, or things like the weather. That's why video games were so appealing. Everything felt easier to control on the screen.

Nico's room, cluttered with gamer cards, piles of graphic t-shirts, snack wrappers, and soda cans, show his commitment to being the best gamer on earth. Or, at least at Sunnyville Elementary School.

"Gotcha!" Nico exclaims as he defeats another boss, pumping his fist in triumph and then pushing his floppy blonde hair

CHAPTER 1
Nico's Real Life

Nico Carmichael was already a gamer at 11-years-old. It's why particular afternoon felt longer as he waited to be dismissed fr Jenkin's fifth grade class. With running through his veins like bolt, Nico sat in anticipation wi from his HD monitor illuminat In just a few minutes, a new up be announced on his favorite vi The world on the screen is whe dominates—where his oppone helpless, and enemies follow hi Of course, the world in real life Nico called it, was a little differ *lot* different. Nico didn't feel as control *anything* in the real worl away from his brow. Smiling, the win sparked a new video idea for his YouTube channel. He knows his followers are going to love this one.

Downstairs, Piper twirls in the living room, her laughter mingling with the sweet melodies she creates on her ukulele. She sings a tune about a heroic quest, inspired by Nico's gaming adventures. Piper's world is one of spotlights and applause, a stark contrast to Nico's domain of high scores and high fives behind the screen. Alfie, their little brother paints on an easel in the kitchen, happily humming along to Piper's song.

"Kids, dinner time!" Mrs. Carmichael calls from the kitchen, her voice wrapping around the house like a warm hug. Mr. Carmichael sets the table, placing each fork and napkin with care.

The scent of spaghetti wafts up the stairs, but Nico is too engrossed in his game to notice. He's so close to breaking his high score, and nothing else seems to matter.

"Hey, hotshot," Mrs. Carmichael appears in Nico's doorway, leaning against the frame with a knowing smile. "Remember that book report? It's due tomorrow. But, come down and eat first."

"Uh-huh," Nico mumbles, his eyes never leaving the screen.

"There's more to life than video games, you know." Her tone is gentle but firm—a quiet reminder of the balance they strive for.

"Sure, Mom," Nico replies, his focus unbroken. He's vaguely aware of the importance of the book report, but the pull of the game is stronger. Just a few more minutes, he tells himself.

As the evening wears on, the house settles into a comforting rhythm: Alfie sleeps sweetly in his room, Piper practices her uke, Mr. and Mrs. Carmichael chat about their day, while Nico dives deeper into his virtual world.

"Goodnight, Nico. Don't stay up too late," Mr. Carmichael pops his head in, his eyebrows raised in a mix of concern and amusement.

"Night, Dad," Nico responds, already lost in another level.

Time slips away, and before he knows it, a yawn stretches across Nico's face. With a final click, he shuts off the game console and realizes the night has claimed the hours meant for his book report.

"Oops," he whispers to the silent room, the weight of the undone assignment settling onto his shoulders. He glances at the clock—bedtime. Panic flutters in his chest, but exhaustion pulls him toward sleep. Tomorrow is another day, but tonight, the adventure ends here. As Nico stands in the middle of his room, a battlefield of scattered papers, game cases, and tangled cords, guilt gnaws at him like hungry worms munching at his insides. He takes a deep breath and springs into action, scooping up the clutter.

"Could've been done with the book report by now," he mumbles to himself, stacking dirty dishes into a neat pile beside his console.

He glances at his backpack leaning on the desk. He slowly collects school papers, books, and his homework planner, before shoving in his game controller by mistake. He then zips it up for the night.

"Good enough," he nods, satisfied with the cleaner space. His bed awaits, promising dreams of high scores and royal battle victories, but the undone book report looms over him, making it difficult to relax.

Climbing under the covers, his mind races. What's he going to say to Miss Jenkin? The thought of facing her without his work complete sends a shiver down his spine. Could he fake a stomachache? Claim the dog ate his book report? No, that won't work; they don't even have a dog.

"Think, Nico, think," he whispers to the darkness.

"Maybe... maybe I can finish it up during recess," he finally concedes, though the idea is as flimsy as tissue paper. With one last nervous glance at his backpack, the unwitting home to his gaming controller, Nico shuts his eyes tight, hoping sleep will offer some escape from the reality of tomorrow's showdown.

CHAPTER 2
No Ordinary Day

"Breakfast time, you two!" Mrs. Carmichael's voice floats up the stairs, tinged with a warmth that only a mother's call can carry. The aroma of freshly baked cinnamon rolls breezes through the halls, seeping under doors and wrapping around corners, enticing Nico to abandon his cozy bed.

He leaps out of bed, hastily scrambling out of his room, eager to be the first one down the stairs. Piper trails behind him with a click-clack of fancy shoes their mother undoubtedly disapproves of for school. They descend the staircase in a half-awake stupor, lured by the promise of sticky, sweet spirals that await them in the kitchen.

"Good morning!" Mrs. Carmichael greets them with a beaming smile. She places a plate piled high with golden-brown cinnamon rolls in the center of the kitchen table, the icing melting into the grooves. Alfie is already at the table devouring the sticky goodness, most of which is covering his face.

"Your favorite, Nico!" she announces, slicing through the calm of the morning with her cheery voice. She leans in, tucking a strand of hair behind Nico's ear as he slides into his seat. "I just know you're going to have the best presentation in the whole class!" Her words, though loving, were uncomfortable. Nico had hoped that his incomplete book report had been a bad dream. Now, it was more real than ever. He desperately wanted to feel heartened by his mom's encouragement, but he felt guilty instead.

Nico tried to enjoy the delicious cinnamon rolls, but the day ahead loomed over him.

His fingers fidget with the edge of his napkin, a shadow of his usual bright-eyed morning self. Mrs. Carmichael tilts her head, studying her son as he offers a sheepish grin in response to her enthusiasm. The corners of his mouth turn up, but the smile doesn't quite reach his eyes. She catches the flicker of something else there—maybe just a case of the pre-presentation jitters.

"Everything okay, honey?" she asks, a hint of concern knitting her brows together.

"Uh-huh," Nico mumbles, his gaze lingering on the swirls of icing atop the cinnamon rolls. His fork pokes at the soft dough, tearing off a tiny bite that he chews slowly, more from obligation than appetite.

Across the table, Piper's plate is already clear, and she's bouncing in her seat, waving her hands with enthusiasm. "Can I have another one, please?" she chirps, her voice bubbling with the same energy as the pop songs she loves to belt out in her room.

"Sure, sweetie," Mrs. Carmichael replies, passing another roll to Piper, who grins with triumph, her fingers sticky with victory.

She then turns back to Nico, who's still playing with his food rather than eating it. "Nico, you've barely touched your breakfast. Aren't you hungry?" Her voice laced with a mix of curiosity and worry, her eyes soft and searching.

Nico shrugs, his shoulders rising and falling like gentle waves. "Not really," he says, pushing the half-eaten roll around his plate. There's an unspoken word hanging in the air, heavy with the weight of uneaten cinnamon rolls and unsaid thoughts.

Mrs. Carmichael reaches over, giving his hand a reassuring squeeze. "You'll do great today," she says, her confidence in him as warm and unwavering as the fresh rolls from the oven. Nico nods, trying to believe it too, even if his stomach feels like it's hosting a butterfly convention.

Nico's eyes drift to the clock on the kitchen wall, its ticking hands nudging him closer to school, to that presentation he's not ready for. Mrs. Carmichael watches her son push in his chair. She knows the look of a kid plotting how to beat the final boss level, and this isn't it. This is different. The untouched cinnamon roll on Nico's plate speaks volumes; when he's excited about something, he eats like he's got a cheat code for unlimited hunger.

"Are you sure you're okay, honey?" she prods gently, but Nico just nods, she lets it go, trusting but still concerned, because mothers have a sixth sense for these things. She knows her boy, and Nico is always hungry—especially for his favorite breakfast.

The bus ride to school feels longer than usual. Piper, seated next to Nico, swings her legs back and forth, her head tilting towards her brother like a sunflower seeking the sun. "You're super quiet today, Nico. What's up?"

Nico hesitates, then leans in closer to Piper, his voice dropping to a whisper. "I didn't finish my project for class," he confesses, the words tumbling out. "I stayed up late gaming and lost track of time."

Piper pats his arm, her face lighting up with an encouraging grin. "Don't sweat it, Nico! You've got the biggest brain I know. You'll come up with something amazing. I'm sure of it!" She believes in him—that's what Piper does best. She's the hype girl, the cheerleader, the one who can find a rainbow in any storm. A rainbow herself in many ways.

Nico wants to believe her, and part of him—a small, flickering part—thinks maybe he can pull off a last-minute save.

When he gets to his classroom, the familiar chaos buzzes around him—pencils scratching, friends chattering, and the lingering smell of freshly copied handouts in the air. But inside his head, it's like someone hit the mute button; he's alone with his thoughts, replaying Piper's encouraging words from the bus ride.

Nico's fingers fumble with the zipper of his backpack as he slides into his desk, the chair squeaking a greeting beneath him. He reaches in, searching for his math book, when his hand brushes against something unexpected—the smooth, cool surface of his game controller. His heart skips a beat. He pulls it out just a smidge, peeks at its familiar buttons, and a smile tugs at the corner of his mouth. It's a strange comfort, this little piece of the gaming world tucked amidst his school supplies, like a hidden level in a familiar game.

"Guess you wanted to come to school too, huh?" he mutters under his breath to the controller, as if it's an old buddy tagging along for an adventure. With a quick glance to make sure no one's watching, he slips his hands around it, thumbs instinctively finding their places on the worn grips.

Nico imagines he's back in his room, the glow of the screen painting his face blue as he navigates among the competition. He's about to try a new move and pull off a win, then—

Zap! The overhead lights in the classroom flicker, casting a stuttering shadow play across the walls. Heads pop up from books, eyes wide with surprise. Nico freezes, his grip tightens on the controller. "No way," he whispers, a flicker of excitement sparking in his chest. Could it be? Did he do that?

"Probably just a power surge," Mrs. Thompson, the science teacher, calls out from the hallway, not even looking up from her papers.

But Nico isn't so sure. He looks down at the controller in his hands, his mind racing. Is it possible? Is there more to this controller than meets the eye? He tucks it away, thinking maybe today won't be so ordinary after all.

Nico's heart pounds like a drum as Miss Jenkin settles into her creaky chair, her eyes scanning the room from behind thick-rimmed glasses. With the stealth of a cat, Nico edges the controller out just a smidge, aiming it at a jar filled with rainbow-colored pencils perched precariously on the corner of her desk.

"Come on," he mumbles under his breath, thumb nudging the button that usually sends his video game characters leaping into action. The air in the room feels charged, expectant.

Clatter! The pencils tumble, scattering across the desk like candy from a pinata. A few roll onto the floor, causing a couple of kids to stifle giggles. Miss Jenkin simply sighs and shakes her head, muttering about gravity.

"Okay, okay," Nico thinks, the wheels in his brain turning faster than skateboard wheels on pavement. "That was kinda cool, but just luck, right?" He couldn't help but wonder.

Lunchtime couldn't come fast enough. As soon as the bell rings, Nico dashes for his lunch box, his mind a bubbling cauldron of what-ifs. He plops down beside Lucas, who's already halfway through a ham sandwich.

"Check this out," Nico whispers, more to himself than to anyone else. He unzips the lunch box and there it is—the peanut butter and jelly sandwich that echoes every mundane mealtime. It looks so...ordinary.

"Time for a little upgrade," he tells the sandwich, only half-believing anything will happen. His fingers curl around the controller, a familiar weight that now teases him with possibilities.

Zap! In a blink, the boring sandwich morphs into a cheesy, delicious slice of pizza, its aroma wafting up as Nico's mouth drops open.

"Whoa! It is me!" he gasps, his voice barely above a whisper, yet giddy with excitement. Magic or not, the controller effortlessly turned lunchtime into showtime, and Nico can't help but feel like he's just unlocked the coolest level yet.

Nico's fingers twitch with exhilaration as he eyes the slice of pizza on his tray, the cheesy edges crisping to a perfect golden brown. Emma slides into the seat next to him, her eyes lighting up at the sight.

"Wow, Nico! Your mom is so cool. She gives you the best lunches." Emma exclaims, leaning in closer.

Nico leans in too, his voice a hushed tone laced with awe and a hint of mischief. "That was a peanut butter and jelly sandwich 10 seconds ago…" he reveals.

Lucas' eyebrows shoot up like twin rockets, his gaze ping-ponging between the pizza and Nico. A smirk plays on Nico's lips as he senses his friend's curiosity reaching new heights. Emma's jaw, practically on the table, was speechless.

"Man, I stayed up way too late gaming last night," Nico confesses, keeping one eye peeled for eavesdroppers. "Didn't even touch my assignment." Lucas and Emma turn to each other in worrisome disbelief, completely ignoring the lunch magic in front of them.

"Wait until you hear this," Nico continues, his voice barely a whisper now, brimming with the thrill of a secret shared. "I brought my game controller to school by accident; I shoved it in my bag with all my stuff. But get this—it might have superpowers."

"Superpowers?" Lucas repeats, skepticism mingling with intrigue in his voice, his eyes narrowing as he processes what he's just heard.

"You're so silly, Nico!" Emma said, chuckling with delight, then taking a bite into her apple slice.

"It's true," Nico nods, a grin spreading across his face as he imagines the endless possibilities. The controller isn't just another gadget; it's a ticket to the unexpected, a gateway to the extraordinary, and he's holding the key.

The air around them seems to crackle with potential as Lucas leans back, crossing his arms, a calculating glint in his eyes. "Show us," Lucas says simply, ready to be convinced.

Nico's heart skips a beat. It's not every day you get to reveal a magic trick—or a newfound power. But with friends like Lucas and Emma watching, ready to dive into the adventure beside him, it feels right. Together, they're about to turn an ordinary school day into something epic.

"Okay…" Nico reaches into his bag and pulls out the controller, holding it out for Emma to see. "But you gotta keep it on the down-low, okay?"

"Cross my heart," Emma says, drawing an 'X' over her chest. "Your secret's locked in the vault."

"Thanks, Em," Nico says, relief washing over him. Lucas nods in agreement, the trio exchanging conspiratorial grins.

"Let's test it out after class," Emma suggests, already brimming with ideas. "I've got a couple of things I wouldn't mind changing with a click of a button."

"Deal," Nico and Lucas say together, sealing their pact with a fist bump. Nico nods, a huge grin spreading across his face, matched by Lucas's own triumphant expression. The three now bound by a secret that has the potential to turn their ordinary school day into an extraordinary adventure.

CHAPTER 3
Sharing the Mystery

When the recess bell sounds, the three friends go outside to test the full potential of the controller. Nico's heart races with excitement as he grips the mysterious controller in his hand, feeling its smooth surface against his skin. His thumbs hovered over the buttons almost as if he could feel the magic oozing out.

"Watch this!" Nico exclaims, eyes gleaming. With a press of a button, he feels a surge of energy ripple through his sneakers.

Lucas, arms crossed, raises an eyebrow, while Emma stands on tiptoes, her red curls bouncing with anticipation. Nico bends his knees, and then—boom! Like a human pogo stick, he soars into the air, higher than the basketball hoop, higher than he ever dreamed possible during a game of foursquare. His laughter echoes across the playground, a mix of glee and disbelief.

"Whoa!" Emma gasps, her hazel eyes wide as saucers.

"Show-off," Lucas smirks, but there's no mistaking the impressed glint in his brown eyes.

Landing with ease, Nico can't help but bask in their astonished faces. But the controller has more tricks up its sleeve. With another press, he darts across the blacktop, a blur faster than any game of freeze tag could allow. Emma claps her hands, cheering him on, while Lucas studies every move, the gears turning in his head.

"Okay, okay, you've got superpowers now," Lucas says, trying to sound unenthusiastic. "Let's see what else it can do."

"Race you to the old oak tree!" Emma calls out, already running with her hair streaming behind her like a fiery comet.

Together, they zigzag through the playground, dodging hopscotch grids and jungle gyms. But it's when they reach the far edge of the school grounds that the real adventure begins. There, where the shadows from the building stretch long and the maintenance shed sits quiet, they find a small gap in the fence, covered by overgrown ivy.

"Never noticed this before," Emma murmurs, her voice tinged with wonder.

"Secret tunnel, secret tunnel!" Nico chants playfully, crouching down to peer through the gap.

Lucas kneels beside him, the thrill of discovery lighting up his face. "This is our spot now. Our secret base."

"Like in the movies!" Emma adds, bubbling with excitement.

They go through the gap, one after another, as the leaves murmur softly to them. Behind the fence, there is a secret garden, a small haven lost to time, with an old swing set and a bench that beckons for stories of the past. It's a wonderland for adventurous fifth-graders—a place to create, to daydream, to become whatever they want to be.

"Can you believe this was here all along?" Nico breathes out, amazed.

"Looks like we're the first to step foot here in ages," Lucas observes, his mind already racing with possibilities.

"Let's make a pact," Emma suggests, her smile warm and trusting. "No matter what happens, this stays our secret."

"Deal," Nico says, extending his hand.

"Deal," Lucas echoes, shaking on it, the mischief in his eyes replaced for a moment with a spark of genuine camaraderie.

In this hidden corner of the world, just beyond the reach of teachers' gazes and school bells, three friends stand together, united by a wondrous secret and the boundless potential of their imaginations.

Nico squats down, the cool grass tickling his palms as he holds the controller like a precious gem. Beside him, Lucas and Emma lean in, their faces bright with curiosity and wonder.

"Imagine all the things we could do with this," Nico says, his voice barely above a whisper.

"Like what?" Emma asks, her pigtails bouncing with each nod of her head.

"Anything!" Nico exclaims. "We could become invisible and eat candy in gym class. Or freeze time during a math quiz!"

"Or see through walls!" Lucas chimes in, chuckling at the thought. "Or change our grades!"

They giggle, the possibilities sprawling out before them like a playground of their wildest dreams. The controller isn't just a toy; it's a key to unlocking a world where they make the rules.

Nico's mind races, thoughts tumbling over one another like excited puppies. His book report looms large in his mind, a beast he's been avoiding, but suddenly, it doesn't seem so scary. Not with the power he holds in his hands.

"Guys, I've got it," Nico announces, standing so quickly that blades of grass cling to his shorts. "I'm going to use this controller to finish my book report!"

Lucas's mouth opens, startled at the thought, while Emma is speechless. They both know Nico well enough to recognize that level of determination. When he gets an idea, there's no stopping him.

"Are you sure it'll work?" Emma asks, her eyebrows knitting together in concern.

"Absolutely." Nico nods with the confidence only a gamer with a magic controller can have. He slips the device into his pocket, already imagining a stellar report, the pride in his mom's eyes making his heart swell.

"Let's keep exploring," he says, eager to test the limits of his new plan. Together, they step further into their secret garden, lost in a world where anything feels possible, and every corner promises a new adventure.

The school bell rings in the distance, bringing the three best friends back to reality. They run full speed back to the double doors, trickling behind their classmates. Nico's shoes make a squeaky noise on the shiny school hall as he hops on his feet, holding the controller in his pocket. It feels like a powerful battery, buzzing his life with new potential.

"Hey, Nico," Lucas says, catching up with a furrow of worry between his brows. "You might want to rethink that book report plan."

Nico slows down, turning to face him. "What? Why?" His own brow crinkles, the idea of finishing that report without stress already a sweet memory he doesn't want to let go of.

"Think about it," Lucas continues, leaning closer and lowering his voice. "What if a teacher catches you? They're always snooping around."

The warning hits Nico harder than a dodgeball during gym class. Teachers have eyes like hawks and noses that can sniff out mischief from a mile away. He imagines Miss Jenkin, with her spectacles perched on her nose, discovering the controller. The thought sends a shiver down his spine.

"Besides," Lucas adds, "they might take it away, and then what? Game over, man."

Nico bites his lip; he knows Lucas has a point. He can already picture the disappointment on his mom's face if he gets caught cheating, even with something as cool as the controller. She's always telling him how proud she is of his honesty, and just thinking about letting her down feels unsettling.

He shifts from one foot to the other, his thoughts racing faster than his legs could ever carry him, even with the controller's help. How would he explain it to his teacher? 'Sorry, I used a magic gadget to do my homework'? Yeah, that wouldn't fly.

"Okay, okay, I hear ya," Nico concedes, though his shoulders slump just a bit. "I'll think of something else."

"Promise?" Emma chimes in, linking arms with both boys. Her voice is like a warm blanket, reminding him that no matter what, they're all in this together.

"Sure," Nico replies, trying to ignore the sinking feeling in his stomach. But deep down, he knows he's not ready to give up on the idea just yet. After all, Nico Carmichael isn't one to back down from a challenge.

CHAPTER 4
The Close Call

The classroom air buzzes with post-recess energy as kids shuffle to their seats, their cheeks still flushed from the playground's escapades. Miss Jenkin taps her glasses up the bridge of her nose and smiles at the parade of students eager to share their book reports. One by one, they stand in front of the class, clutching their index cards like lifelines.

Nico, with his tousled blonde hair, leans back in his chair, his blue eyes tracking each presenter. He's not nervous, nope, not Nico. He's got this—after all, he's conquered much tougher levels on his favorite games, and this is just another quest on life's adventure map.

"Remember to speak clearly and share your favorite part," Miss Jenkin reminds them, her voice a gentle nudge.

A boy with a dog-eared book about dinosaurs takes his turn, and Nico can't help but be whisked away on a daydream about prehistoric mammals surviving epic laser battles. But the ticking clock above the whiteboard pulls him back to Room 118. It's just ten minutes until the bell rings for music class, and Nico feels that familiar itch—a mix of excitement and impatience—as time ticks closer to his own moment in the spotlight.

He fidgets with the hem of his T-shirt, tapping his foot to an inaudible rhythm. Nerves seem to take over, swallowing him in a frenzy of anxiety, doubt, and hopefulness. Waiting as patiently as possible, he watches the hands of the clock tick, his mind already humming with the missions he'll complete—both in the classroom and in the boundless realms of his imagination.

Suddenly pulled from his daydream by the sound of Miss Jenkin, she turns to him saying, "Nico, you are up," then gives him an encouraging nod.

Nico stands, his palms sweaty. He's ready, or at least that's what he tells himself as he braces for the short walk to the front of the room. His fingers curl around the controller, a familiar comfort against the jitters nipping at his nerves.

As he strides past rows of desks, Nico catches Emma and Lucas's eyes. He flashes them a confident grin and mouths the words, "I got this." The corners of his mouth tick upwards into a daring smile, the thrill of performance sparking in his eyes.

Lucas leans forward, eyes narrowed in silent calculation, while Emma offers a supportive, almost protective glance. But it's the object in Nico's grasp that draws their focus. The controller, snug in his hand, seems out of place amidst the pencils and notebooks scattered across the desks. Both Lucas and Emma had hoped that Nico wouldn't try to use the controller, but now they hoped their daring friend wouldn't get caught.

Nico reaches the front, turning to face his audience, his classmates. He takes a deep breath, ready to dive into the world of his book report, controller and all. It's more than just a piece of plastic and buttons to him—it's an anchor to the worlds he loves to explore. And today, it's the bridge between his two favorite adventures: the tales within pages and the quests on the screen.

Emma's hazel eyes dart to Lucas, an unspoken worry passing between them. They hold their breath in a mirror of concern as they watch Nico take center stage.

"Mr. Carmichael," Miss Jenkin begins, her voice steady and commanding the room's attention, "why do you have a game controller with you?"

Nico's hands tighten around the plastic casing, his thumb brushing over the buttons he knows so well. With a half-cocked smile, he lifts the controller slightly. "Oh, um. This? It's my good luck charm," he says, voice wavering just enough to betray his anxiety.

Miss Jenkin purses her lips thoughtfully, the faint lines around her mouth deepening. "I appreciate a bit of superstition now and then," she concedes, the ghost of a smile flickering across her face. "However, it looks like a distraction to me." She points toward his desk at the back of the room. "Please return it to your desk, Nico."

Nico's emotions do a somersault. The controller feels heavier now, like it's suddenly filled with lead instead of circuits and wires. He nods slowly, trying to mask his disappointment with a brave face. The controller has been more than just a good luck charm; it's been his sidekick in countless adventures. But rules are rules, even for heroes.

Nico's feet feel glued to the colorful classroom carpet as he stares at the controller in his hand, its familiar shape now a symbol of his sinking hopes. Each step back to his desk feels like his legs are slime and his feet are covered in mud, his mind racing with the thought that without his trusty digital sidekick, his report will be incomplete. He imagines the red F glaring up at him from Miss Jenkin's grade book, and it sends a shiver down his spine.

"Come on, Nico, you've got this," he whispers to himself, trying to ignore the thumping of his heart against his ribs. He reaches his desk, the wood etched with names of students past, and unzips his backpack with shaky fingers. The controller slips into the dark cavity of his bag, hidden away like a secret treasure.

Lucas, eyes sharp as eagle talons, watches for the perfect moment. As Miss Jenkin turns to scribble something on the whiteboard, his hand darts out quick as lightning. "I got you," he murmurs to Nico under his breath, snatching the controller from the depths of Nico's backpack. Lucas's smirk is barely concealed as he tucks the device into his own jacket pocket, the weight of his cunning plan settling comfortably against his chest.

Nico glances over, his piercing blue eyes meeting Lucas's expressive brown ones. A silent nod passes between them, an unspoken pact of mischief and mutual need for the other's success. Nico can't help but feel a flicker of hope rekindle within him.

Lucas's fingers curl around the edges of the controller, a feeling of power surging through him as he imagines steering Nico's presentation to victory. He leans back in his chair, a sly glint in his eye, already picturing the applause that will surely follow their secret teamwork. This little piece of technology is more than just buttons—it's their ticket to the top. A way for control of the unknown.

"Trust me," Lucas mouths across the room to Nico, who's nervously biting his lip at the front of the class. The plan seems foolproof, a perfect save for what could have been a sinking ship.

But as soon as Lucas hits the power button, the unexpected happens. The controller shudders in his hand like it's alive, the plastic exterior suddenly too warm against his skin. Lucas frowns, a flicker of worry crossing his face. "Come on, don't fail me now," he mutters under his breath.

The buttons begin to twitch, and the controller emits a series of peculiar hums and beeps, as if it's speaking a language only it understands. Lucas's heart hammers with unease, his ambitious plans teetering on the edge of disaster.

"Work, you silly thing!" Lucas urges, giving the controller a gentle shake. But it's no use; the device seems to have a mind of its own. It grows hotter, almost burning, and Lucas yelps, the heat biting at his palms. With a jolt of alarm, he lets go. The controller tumbles out of his grasp, now an unpredictable force outside anyone's control.

Nico's eyes widen from the front of the class, and Emma, who has been watching the whole scene unfold, claps a hand over her mouth. The students' attention shifts from the front of the room to the commotion in the back, curious whispers bubbling up around the room.

"Is everything okay?" Miss Jenkin asks, turning away from the whiteboard with a puzzled look on her face.

"Uh, yeah, all good," Lucas stammers, cheeks flushed with a mix of embarrassment and shock, trying to act natural despite the chaos. He shoots Nico a reassuring glance, hoping to salvage what's left of their plan without letting on to the wild ride the controller had just taken them on.

The controller plummets, a casualty of Lucas's searing grip, and crashes to the classroom floor with an ominous crack. Gasps echo around the room as all eyes dart toward the unexpected sound. Nico's heart leaps into his throat; that's not just any controller—it's his free pass to acing this book report.

"Oops!" Someone in the back can't help but mutter, and a ripple of nervous giggles spreads like the wave at a ball game.

Nico doesn't miss a beat. He bolts from the front, pushing past his desk chair with a clatter. His sneakers screech against the linoleum as he skids to a stop where his beloved controller lies in pieces. The other kids crane their necks, murmuring among themselves, while Miss Jenkin looks on, bewildered by the sudden commotion.

"Be okay, be okay," Nico pleads under his breath, the words barely a whisper.

He scoops up the fragments, cradling them in his small hands as if they're more fragile than a bird's egg. A collective hush falls over the classroom, the air thick with anticipation. Then something magical happens—right before their wide, disbelieving eyes, the broken pieces wiggle and twitch. They snap together with a series of soft clicks, the cracks sealing as if guided by an unseen force.

"Whoa..." escapes from someone in the crowd.

With a final shudder, the controller begins to glow, radiating a warm light that bathes Nico's anxious face. Its buttons flicker back to life, each one illuminated and inviting. In Nico's hands, it's no longer just a piece of plastic and circuitry; it's a symbol of hope, of untapped potential.

"Neat trick," whispers Emma, her tone a mix of awe and concern, while Lucas just nods, relief washing over him.

Miss Jenkin clears her throat, ready to restore order, but for a moment longer, the room remains captivated by the spectacle of the mended controller and the boy who holds it, both seemingly invincible.

The warmth from the glowing controller ebbs away as Miss Jenkin steps forward, her hands on her hips and her stare fixed firmly on Nico.

"Class," she begins, her voice cutting through the lingering wonder like a knife, "we've had quite enough excitement for one afternoon." She glances at the wall clock, then back to Nico, whose heart sinks like a stone in a pond. "It's clear we're not going to have time for any more presentations today."

Nico's shoulders droop, but he can't help the tiny flicker of relief that sparks within him. He clutches the controller tighter, his good luck charm that feels more like a lifeline now.

Miss Jenkin points a stern finger at the mystical device in Nico's grasp. "Nico, that controller of yours caused quite the stir. I must insist you leave it at home tomorrow. If you bring it back to class, I'm afraid I'll have to take it."

"Take it?" Nico repeats, his voice barely above a whisper, but the alarm bells ring loud in his head. The thought of being separated from the magic, even for a day, sends a shiver down his spine.

"Rules are rules," Miss Jenkin says with a firm nod, leaving no room for argument.

A heavy sigh escapes Nico as he nods in understanding. The controller, still pulsating with a soft glow, seems to pulse in agreement, its light dimming in resignation. He tucks it away into his backpack, feeling as though he's locking away a piece of himself.

"Tomorrow, Nico," Miss Jenkin adds, a hint of kindness returning to her voice. "Make sure you're ready to present your book report."

With those words, the spell is broken. The classroom bursts back to life with the rustle of papers and the shuffle of feet, each student already buzzing about the day's unusual events. Nico catches Emma's sympathetic glance, and Lucas gives him a reassuring pat on the shoulder. They're in this together, come what may.

When the final school bell of the day rings with a cheerful chime, and kids swarm out of the classroom like bees from a hive, Nico trails behind, his backpack slung over one shoulder. He's got that funny feeling in his stomach—not quite butterflies, more like power-ups jumping around. It's relief. Sweet, sweet relief.

He promises, right there in the noisy hallway with lockers clanging shut, that he'll dive into his book report as soon as he gets home. No distractions. This report is going to be epic, he tells himself.

"Hey, Nico!" Emma calls out, weaving through the crowd with Lucas at her side. They catch up to him, their faces bright with the kind of bond that only a shared secret can forge. "You're okay, right?" Emma asks, concern flickering in her eyes.

"Totally," Nico says, flashing a confident grin. "Tonight, I'm gonna work on my report. Tomorrow, Miss Jenkin won't even remember the controller incident."

Lucas bumps fists with Nico. "That's the spirit! And if you need any help, just holler. We'll make it a mission!"

"Thanks, guys." Nico feels the warmth of friendship wrapping around him like a superhero's cape. With pals like these, who needs a lucky controller?

They step out into the golden afternoon light, where parents are waiting and school buses rumble. As they part ways, Nico's steps feel lighter. He's got this. After all, every hero faces trials, but it's the quest that makes the story worth telling. Nico walks the familiar path home, already plotting out the twists and turns of his book report. It's going to be one for the books—pun totally intended.

CHAPTER 5
Doing the Work

That night, Nico Carmichael sprawls across his bedroom floor, surrounded by a fortress of colored pencils and construction paper. He feels a warm, fizzy sense of pride bubbling up inside him because tonight, there are no fibs to tell Mom, no secret levels to conquer—just him and his project.

His mom had peeked in earlier, beaming at him actually doing homework for once, which only made that fizzy feeling fizzier. The clock ticks away, its soft, rhythmic sounds a reminder that Monday nights are different. No trampoline shoes, no balancing acts or back handsprings. Just him and the quiet, except for the tick-tick-ticking that seems to whisper, "Think, Nico, think."

Nico's hands move automatically, attaching the various parts of his book report to the poster board and writing details under each picture. Occasionally, his thoughts creeped back to the controller. It's just sitting there, on his desk, innocent and yet so full of mystery.

"Maybe it's alien technology," he speculates, adjusting a notecard. The idea sends a shiver down his spine, thrilling and terrifying. Or, perhaps it's a new design from some secret government agency? Or a prototype from a video game company that accidentally fell out of someone's backpack and into mine? Nico sat curious, wondering what made the controller act the way it did and why it chose him.

"Could be worth millions..." he whispers to himself, a grin spreading across his face. And then he giggles because, come on, it's probably just a broken controller, right? But still, there's that maybe, that what if, and it's as tantalizing as the final level of his favorite game.

"Focus, Nico," he tells himself, glancing between his project and the mysterious controller. There's time tonight, plenty of it, to ponder over possibilities and dream up theories. After all, Nico Carmichael loves to dream big. And with that, his project was almost complete. As the last sentence of his essay takes shape, a sense of accomplishment washes over him. He's done it; the assignment is complete, and there's still time before bed. A reward is in order—video game time!

With fingers wrapped over the controller, a sense of unease mixed with curiosity prickled his skin. How did it snap like a twig when Lucas touched it, but now it's as solid as a rock? He turns the controller over in his hands, searching for any sign of damage, any clue that could explain the mystery. But it remains stubbornly perfect, its buttons shiny and unscathed.

He boots up his console, the screen coming to life with vibrant colors and inviting sounds. For a while, he loses himself in digital worlds, guiding his character through quests and battles with the practiced ease of an expert gamer. Laughter bubbles up from within as he dodges pixelated foes and racks up points.

But even as he plays, part of his mind keeps drifting back to the controller. What secrets does it hold? And why him? Why did it end up in his hands?

With a yawn, Nico decides those questions can wait for another day. For now, it's enough to enjoy the simple pleasure of a game well played and a Monday night well spent. He saves his progress, switches off the console, and tucks himself into bed, the controller's enigma bookmarked in his mind for tomorrow.

Nico heads downstairs to the kitchen for a glass of chocolate milk. His mom stands at the sink rinsing dishes—a hint of burger night still lingering in the air.

"Hey, Mom," Nico chirps, his voice carrying the lightness of his mood. "You know what would be amazing? If we woke up to the smell of cinnamon rolls tomorrow. Just saying."

Mrs. Carmichael turns, a smile tugging at the corners of her mouth. "Is that so?" She raises an eyebrow, the playful glint in her eyes matching Nico's own mischief. "Well, I might just have to consider it. But only if someone helps me with the icing."

"You got it!" Nico says, already picturing the warm, gooey pastries fresh out of the oven. He imagines drizzling the sweet, creamy icing on top, his mouth watering at the thought of truly enjoying it this time around.

"Good night, sweetie," Mrs. Carmichael says, giving him a loving hug. "Don't let the bed bugs bite."

"Or the sugar plums dance too much," Nico adds with a grin, turning toward the hallway. As he heads off to his room, happy thoughts fill his dreams—both the kind with high scores and victories on his console and the sugary kind waiting for him in the morning

CHAPTER 6
Master of Possibilities

The next day, Nico stands in front of the classroom, nervously clutching the edges of his report, the white paper almost crumpling under his grip. With a deep breath and a glance at Miss Jenkin's encouraging nod, he begins. His voice shakes at first, but as he dives into the book report, it steadies. He expressively describes the book and the main characters with ease, accentuating his knowledge of the challenges they face, and how they always help each other out.

"…and that's why I found this book to be so exciting," Nico concludes, pushing hair out of his eyes with a triumphant flick. "It's a story about friendship and bravery!"

The room erupts into applause, the sound washing over Nico and bouncing off the colorful posters on the walls. Miss Jenkin beams at him from behind her desk, her hands coming together in enthusiastic claps. Nico's cheeks glow a shade of pink, the kind that only shows up when he feels both embarrassed and proud.

As the clapping fades and Nico makes his way back to his seat, he can't help but let a smile creep onto his face. He slides into his chair beside Emma, who gives him a thumbs-up. "That was awesome!" she whispers.

"Thanks," he replies, the relief clear in his voice. He had been given an extension on the book report—his own personal disaster turned lucky break.

Sitting there, surrounded by his friends and still feeling the echo of applause in his bones, Nico makes a silent promise to himself. No more last-minute panics, no more relying on luck to get through his assignments. He'd seen how good it felt to be prepared, to be recognized for his hard work. From now on, he will plan better, work smarter, and never take such a chance again.

He glances down at his backpack where the mysterious controller is hidden away, its buttons holding secrets and wonders he has yet to fully explore. For a moment, he's tempted to tell Emma and Lucas about his latest discovery, but he hesitates. This magic, this unexpected twist in his otherwise ordinary life, was something extraordinary—but it also felt delicate, like a soap bubble that might pop if handled too roughly.

Instead, Nico focuses on the here and now, the warmth of success still lingering in the air. He'd given a great book report, and that was all on him—no magic needed. And for a fifth grader with a passion for video games and a YouTube channel waiting for his next big break, that was a pretty cool feeling indeed.

Nico, Emma, and Lucas spill out onto the playground, a jumble of energy and laughter. The sun is beaming down, casting a glow on the hopscotch lines and the monkey bars that seem to dare them for another climb. Nico was happy with his work, but now recess has its own brand of excitement.

"Hey, Nico," Emma calls out, her red curls bouncing as she skips over to him. "Could your controller give me a new style?" Her hazel eyes sparkle with mischief. She twirls a strand of hair around her finger. "I want all new clothes to match Willow!"

"Yea, yea, and I want to look like Marshmello!" Lucas chimes in, grinning wide. His spiky brown hair seems to stand at attention, just like his personality—

always ready for a challenge or a chance to stir things up.

"Very funny," Emma says, not missing a beat. She rolls her eyes and reaches for the controller that Nico just pulled out, her fingers brushing against the cool, mysterious device. But something strange happens the moment her hands wrap around it—the power flickers and fades. The screen that normally glows bright goes dark, and the buttons don't even blink. It's as if the controller decides to take a nap right there in Emma's hands.

"Uh-oh," Nico mumbles, peering over Emma's shoulder. The playground buzzes around them, kids chasing soccer balls and swapping collectible cards, oblivious to the tiny crisis unfolding by the swings. Emma's warm eyes meet Nico's, both filled with questions and a sliver of worry. What type of magic had they stumbled upon, and why did it decide to play hide and seek now?

Nico scratches his head, trying to figure out this latest twist. There's something about that controller, something unpredictable and wild. He wonders what adventure—or maybe what trouble—it will take them on next.

Lucas's face turns the color of a ripe tomato as he glares at Emma, his brown eyes narrowing. "You broke it!" he accuses, jabbing a finger toward the lifeless controller in her hands.

Emma's cheeks flush, but she stands her ground, red curls bouncing as she shakes her head firmly. "Oh, like you broke it yesterday?" she retorts, her voice laced with frustration. Her stare fiery, not willing to take the blame so easily.

"Okay, okay, let's just calm down," Nico intervenes, trying to smooth things over. He reaches out, his fingers gently prying the controller from Emma's grasp. The moment it touches his palm, the device springs back to life, its screen glowing warmly under the afternoon sun.

"Works fine," Nico announces with a small shrug as he curiously examines the suddenly resurrected controller.

"Let me try," Lucas insists, snatching the controller from Nico's hold. But no sooner does it rest in his hands than a troubling sound emerges. A crackle sizzles through the air, followed by a sharp hiss that makes everyone's hair stand on end.

"What the-?" Lucas yelps, startled. The controller feels like it's about to burst into flames right there in his grip. Reflexively, he drops it onto the ground where it lands with a thud, the ominous noises abruptly stopping as if the device decides to hold its breath.

Nico, Emma, and Lucas exchange glances, speechless. They all know something bizarre is going on with the controller — something beyond the realm of normal fifth-grade recess shenanigans.

"Hey! Stop it!" Nico's voice cuts through the tension. He lunges for the controller, dust puffing up from where it lies abandoned on the playground gravel. His fingers curl around the cool plastic, and instantly, as if greeting an old friend, the device buzzes to life in his hands.

The tiny screen lights up with vibrant colors that dance across Nico's face, reflecting a kaleidoscope of possibilities. He holds it up, a triumphant grin spreading across his face. "Yes! Well, I guess it's trying to tell us that I'm the only one it likes," he says, almost apologetically but with a hint of pride. "Sorry guys."

Nico's friends can't hide their disappointment, their shoulders drooping. But there's an unspoken understanding that this mysterious controller and Nico have a connection.

Emma puts her hands on her hips, a gesture sparking with the sort of injustice only a playground dispute can ignite. She glances at Lucas, who mirrors her frown, his calculating gaze shifting to the glowing device in Nico's hands and back again.

"Hey, that's not fair," Emma protests, her voice tinged with a whine that even she didn't expect. The red curls framing her face bounce as she juts out her hip, hands finding the comfort of her denim jacket pockets.

"Yea, make it work for us, too!" Lucas chimes in, his tone edging on a demand rather than a request. He crosses his arms over his chest, standing like a miniature superhero minus the cape, but with all the entitlement.

Nico looks between his two friends, the controller snug in his grasp. It almost hums with a sense of loyalty to him alone, and for a moment, he feels a twinge of guilt mixed with an electric buzz of exclusivity.

Nico shrugs, the controller snug in his pocket now, its mysterious allure tucked away. "Look, I can't explain it. I don't know what it can and can't do," he admits, his voice steady despite the tension between them. He scans his friends obvious feelings of disappointment, then breaks into a boyish grin that crinkles the corners of his eyes.

"Hey, anybody want to see me do an aerial into a back handspring?" he asks, eager to shift the mood. His eyes sparkle with the same energy that fuels his endless YouTube video ideas.

"Sure!" Emma responds first, her earlier frustration dissolving into curiosity. She knows Nico's flips are almost as good as any magic show.

"Yeah, bro. Show us what you got, Nico!" Lucas adds, forgetting the controller for a moment as he anticipates the display of acrobatics.

The playground becomes their stage, gravel crunching underfoot as Nico steps back, giving himself room. In one swift motion, he launches into the air. His body twists and turns, a blur of movement against the bright blue sky. Emma and Lucas watch, their mouths agape, as Nico lands firmly on his feet, arms raised triumphantly.

"Whoa! That was awesome!" Lucas shouts, clapping his hands, caught up in the excitement.

"Again, again!" Emma cheers with amazement.

Nico can't help but beam at his friends' reactions. The controller wasn't working for them, but his gymnastics tricks? They were always surefire hits.

Moments pass as the children wait in anticipation for Nico's next trick. He clutches the device close, like a secret charm. With a deep breath, the blond-haired athlete springs into action, launching himself skyward as if propelled by invisible rockets.

"Whoa!" a kid from the monkey bars gasps, pointing at Nico's soaring form.

Nico ascends, higher and higher, a human comet streaking through an expanse of blue.

The world below seems to hold its breath, playground chatter fading into awestruck silence. He flips—a perfect aerial—his body spinning with such grace that it defies gravity. Then comes the back handspring, executed farther and faster than any before, a blur of limbs and laughter.

"Did you see that?" Lucas exclaims, his voice a blend of disbelief and pure excitement.

Emma nods, her eyes wide as frisbees, "He's flying!"

Cheers erupt from every corner of the playground. Children abandon their games and huddle closer, drawn by the spectacle of Nico's fearless acrobatics. Each flip is a burst of energy, each twist a thread weaving him into the fabric of schoolyard legend.

"Go, Nico!" the chorus of young voices chants, a symphony of encouragement that buoys him to even greater heights.

The fifth grader is in his element, fueled by the cheers and the mysterious power of the controller. Trick after trick spills from him effortlessly—cartwheels that turn into double back handsprings, leaps that seem to snatch the clouds from the sky. Every move is more extreme than the last, Nico's world reduced to the thrill of motion and the echo of his friends' laughter. He felt like somebody who mattered. For the first time ever, he was popular, adored, and everyone finally knew his name.

"Amazing!" Emma squeals, clapping her hands together.

"Unbelievable!" Lucas adds, a grin splitting his face.

Nico lands one final, breathtaking maneuver, the ground shaking beneath the force of his arrival. He stands there, chest heaving, a conqueror bathed in the glow of midday sun and childhood glory. His peers circle around him, their energy palpable, their admiration clear in their stares and relentless applause.

"Encore, encore!" they cheer, not yet ready for the magic to end.

And Nico, ever the showman, can't resist the call. With the controller snug in his pocket, he readies himself for another round of gasps and cheers. Today, on this playground stage, he's not just any ordinary kid—he's a superhero, a wizard, a star born from the dreams of every 11-year-old who ever longed to fly.

As Nico lands his final flip, dust from the playground swirls around him like a cloak of victory. The crowd of kids is wild, their cheers bouncing off the school walls. But it's not just the students who are captivated by Nico's dazzling display. From the edge of the concrete, Mr. Bell, the principal with his ever-present bow tie and funky glasses, strides forward, phone out ready to record a video.

"Whoa," Nico mutters under his breath, eyes widening as he spots the principal.

"Absolutely outstanding!" Mr. Bell exclaims, his voice barely heard over the chants and claps. He fumbles with his smartphone, tapping at it with a sense of urgency. A grin tugs at the corner of his mouth as he raises the device to capture Nico's next feat.

"Hey, everyone, let's give it up for Nico!" Mr. Bell shouts, turning his phone to record the reactions of the amazed onlookers. "We certainly have a star here at our elementary school. Bravo, Nico Carmichael!"

The kids erupt into another round of applause, spurred on by Mr. Bell's enthusiasm. Nico feels a surge of pride, a thrill of excitement tingling through his limbs. This is more than he could have ever imagined, and all thanks to the controller that seems to be an extension of himself. So this is what it feels like to be 'cool', he thought.

"So sorry to be a party pooper here, but back to class, everyone!" Miss Jenkin calls out with a friendly wave, her voice cutting through the exhilaration.

Nico bounces towards the line forming to head back inside, the mysterious controller snug against his side. High fives fly his way, each one a jolt of joy. Laughter peppers the air as hands reach out to pat his back—some gentle, some a bit too enthusiastic.

"Good job, dude!" Lucas says, his grin matching the brightness of the day.

"Wow, Nico, you were amazing!" Emma adds, her words lifting him even higher.

"Thanks, guys!" Nico replies, trying to keep his casual cool. But inside, his heart races; he's soaring without even leaving the ground. Thanks to the controller, he feels invincible, like a superstar among his peers.

They file back into the school, a buzz of energy trailing behind them. Nico's already thinking about what else this controller can do—the possibilities stretch out like the endless blue sky above their heads.

The rumor mill whirls at warp speed through the halls of Sunnyville Elementary, and by the time the final bell rings, Nico Carmichael's name is on the tip of every tongue. "Did you see Nico's flips?" one kid whispers to another. "He's like a superhero or something," another responds with awe in his voice.

Nico strolls through the corridors with an air of newfound confidence, his backpack slung over one shoulder as classmates throw him admiring glances and nods. The controller, tucked safely in his pocket, feels warm against his thigh—a secret source of his sudden fame.

"Hey, Nico!" a girl calls out as she catches up to him, her ponytail swinging. "That trick today was epic!"

"Thanks," Nico replies, a small, proud smile playing on his lips. He can't help but bask in the glow of the attention all day.

Even under the hum of the cafeteria chatter and the clanging of trays, Nico had plans to spice things up.

"Ugh, not sloppy joes again," groans Lucas, crinkling his nose at the sight of the usual Wednesday fare.

But as Nico's classmates reach the front of the line, their grumbles turn into gasps of delight. Where once sat a mountain of mushy buns and ground beef, there are now golden mounds of crispy French fries and succulent chicken nuggets. The air fills with the sound of high-fives and laughter as they heap their trays with the unexpected feast.

"Did you do this, Nico?" Emma asks, eyes widening as she grabs an extra handful of fries.

"Maybe I did, maybe I didn't," Nico says with a wink, enjoying the buzz of excitement his little stunt creates. After all, who could say no to a surprise fast-food fiesta?

Later that week, Nico's newfound knack for making school cooler takes another leap forward. It's a particularly hot Thursday, and the sun beats down on the playground like a relentless oven. As kids line up for a drink, Nico casually leans against the wall, sipping his secret: lemonade, sweet and cold, from the water fountain.

"Whoa! Is that lemonade?" exclaims a thirsty classmate, as others catch on and start pressing their own cups against the magical tap.

"Best water fountain ever!" someone shouts, and a chorus of agreement ripples through the crowd.

The fun doesn't stop there. Back in their classroom, where multiplication tables haunt the walls like arithmetic ghosts, Nico faces a new challenge. Pop quiz Thursday—the dreaded surprise test that sends shivers down every fifth-grader's spine.

"Open your quizzes, and remember, no books or notes allowed," Miss Jenkin announces with her usual sternness.

A collective groan fills the room. But Nico, cool as an ice pop, slips his hand into his pocket and thumbs the controller. In a flash, Miss Jenkin's voice mellows.

"Actually, let's make it an open book test," she decides, much to everyone's shock.

"Seriously?" Lucas mouths across the room.

"Shh," Emma shushes him, already flipping her textbook open to the right page.

As pencils scratch and pages turn, Nico leans back in his chair, satisfied. With his magic controller, school isn't just easy—it's a blast. And as for being the hero of the hour? Well, that's just the cherry on top.

Nico scoots through the hallway, his backpack bouncing against his shoulders, a grin plastered on his face that just won't quit. He's riding high on a wave of whispers and giggles that trail behind him like the tail of a comet. The magic controller, tucked safely in his pocket, remains a secret source of never-ending surprises.

"Did you see Nico's flip on the playground?" one kid says to another as they pass by lockers adorned with stickers and magnets.

"Totally! And he aced the spelling bee without even studying!" another chimes in, eyes wide with awe.

At his locker, his friends cluster around him, their faces lit up with anticipation. Emma leans in close, her voice a hushed excitement. "What are you going to do today?"

Nico shrugs, feigning nonchalance, but the twinkle in his eyes gives him away. "Who knows? Maybe I'll turn math class into a video game."

"Can you make homework disappear too?" Lucas jokes, nudging Nico's arm with a hopeful grin.

"Maybe," Nico teases back, the wheels in his head turning faster than a fidget spinner.

When the bell rings, signaling the end of the day, a ripple of relief spreads through the room. Children stuff their books into bags and chat about after-school plans. But for Nico, the real fun is just beginning. With each step he takes, leaving a trail of laughter and mischief in his wake, it's clear—he's not just a fifth grader anymore. He's a legend in the making.

Throughout the week, the magic of the controller keeps the spotlight firmly on Nico. Each day, he steps into school decked out in new threads—cool graphic tees and expensive sneakers that make his friends drool with envy. "Looking sharp, dude!" Lucas exclaims one morning, eyeing Nico's fresh outfit.

Homework, which used to be the bane of his existence, now becomes a breeze. With the controller by his side, Nico completes assignments with such ease that even Mrs. Pennington, the stern math teacher, raises an eyebrow in surprise. "Very impressive work, Mr. Carmichael," she remarks as she hands back a test adorned with a bright red A.

And then there are the gym classes. Once the place where Nico felt most out of his element, now he dominates the games, leaping higher and running faster than ever before. His classmates cheer as he scores goal after goal during soccer, leaving the other team in a daze.

"Is there anything you can't do?" Emma asks one afternoon as they walk off the field, her tone a mix of admiration and curiosity.

"Guess I'm just having a good week," Nico shrugs, though his heart swells with pride, making him the legend of Sunnyville Elementary.

CHAPTER 7
Epic Field Trip

Nico shows off one of his favorite gamer dances as he joins the line of classmates outside the school. His feet dance across the pavement buzzing with the kind of excitement that only a field trip can bring. The chatter among students of wild guesses about what they'll see at the science museum and stories of last year's trip to the zoo – which, by all accounts, had been epic.

"Think there'll be robot dinosaurs?" a classmate asks, wide-eyed and hopeful.

"Or maybe a black hole you can look into!" another chimes in, gesturing wildly as if he might fall into an imaginary void right there on the sidewalk.

The science museum is like a giant playground for someone as curious as Nico. Today could be extra special, he thinks, fingers brushing against the familiar shape of his controller through the fabric of his backpack.

He'd debated with himself all morning, the controller sitting on his desk like a silent challenge. Should it stay or should it go? In the end, the lure of potential mischief had won out. It's not every day you get to roam the halls filled with exhibits that could come alive with just the right touch of a button.

"Hey, Nico, you think they'll have new video game tech there?" one of his classmates nudges him, snapping him back to the moment.

"Maybe," Nico replies, the corner of his mouth tilting up. "I guess we'll find out."

With a final pat to his backpack, assuring himself the controller is still safely tucked inside, Nico steps forward as the line begins to move. Today, the museum won't know what hit it. And neither will his classmates if his plan works out. He can hardly wait to see the looks on their faces.

After what seems like forever and an hour, the school bus rumbles to a stop in front of the museum. As he steps off the bus, Nico's sneakers hit the sidewalk with an eager thud. Excitement buzzes through him like electricity as he joins the sea of classmates spilling out onto the sidewalk in front of the science museum.

"Whoa, look at that line!" Emma exclaims, pointing toward the throng of kids stretching around the block.

"Must be every fifth grader in the state," Lucas mutters, craning his neck to see the end.

Nico's eyes widen behind his glasses as he surveys the crowd—a colorful tapestry of backpacks and laughter. They all seem drawn here by the same magnetic pull of curiosity. But unlike them, Nico has an ace up his sleeve—or rather, in his backpack.

"Come on," he urges Emma and Lucas, weaving through clumps of students from other schools. Their chatter blends into a buzzing soundtrack for their adventure, snippets of conversation about science projects and favorite dinosaurs drifting past Nico's ears.

He spots the banner draped across the museum entrance, its bold letters announcing the new dinosaur exhibit. The image of a towering T-Rex sends a ripple of excitement through the crowd. Nico can almost hear its mighty roar echoing from the past, calling tourists from miles away to stand beneath its bones.

"Bet it's going to be packed inside," Lucas says, frowning at the thought of jostling for a view of the exhibits.

"Doesn't matter," Nico replies, patting his backpack again. His fingertips brush against the controller, and he feels a tingle of anticipation. Today, he'll make sure they have the best field trip ever. After all, who needs to worry about crowds when you've got a little bit of magic waiting to be unleashed?

Nico squints at the never-ending snake of kids zigzagging in front of the museum. They inch forward like a slow-moving caterpillar, and his heart sinks. Waiting is not part of today's plan. He can already picture the cool fossils and ancient bones just beyond those doors, but with this crowd, he might spend half the day staring at the back of someone's head instead.

"Ugh, we'll never get in at this rate," Emma mutters, her shoulders slumping.

"Unless..." Nico trails off, his brain clicking into gear. There's a sparkle of mischief in his eyes as he slips his hand into his backpack. The controller feels like a secret key in his grasp, and his thumb hovers over the buttons. With a quick press here and another there, he makes his move—hoping for something, anything, to cut this line down to size.

"Whoa, did you guys feel that?" Lucas suddenly asks, his eyes wide.

Before they know it, the chattering sea of students part and Miss Jenkin's class strides through, bypassing the queue entirely. It's as if an invisible force clears the way, and Nico's classmates thrilled with excitement, remain unaware of the quiet hero with the controller in his pocket.

"Look!" Emma exclaims, tugging at Nico's sleeve. "Isn't that—"

It sure is. Standing by the entrance, with a lanyard around his neck and a smile on his face, is none other than Tommy Paris—the YouTuber himself. His presence instantly draws a crowd of gawking fans and subscribers.

"Good morning, everyone! I'm Tommy Paris, your guide for today," the popular YouTuber says, his voice familiar to everyone who watches his videos. "Ready to have some fun?"

Nico can't believe their luck. Not only are they first in line, but they've also scored the coolest tour guide in the history of field trips. High-fives fly through the air as his classmates gather around their famous guide, ready to take on the museum with endless enthusiasm.

"Best. Day. Ever," Nico whispers to himself. His friends nod in agreement, unaware of the little gadget that's just turned an ordinary outing into an extraordinary adventure.

Nico's heart races with the thrill of the unexpected as he trails behind his classmates, led by the magnificent Tommy Paris through the echoing halls of the science museum. With each step, the buzz of excitement from his friends combined with the magic of the controller in his backpack feels like a secret superpower fueling their adventure. The whispers and eagerness from other kids in line only amplify Nico's feeling of triumph. He's the reason everyone is having a great time; he's the mastermind behind the best field trip ever.

"Next up, the universe awaits us," Tommy announces with a gesture grand enough to sweep them all into orbit, leading the way toward the museum's planetarium.

The dimly lit dome of the planetarium swallows them whole, stars twinkling above like distant promises. As they settle onto the plush seats, Nico sneaks a hand into his backpack and wraps his fingers around the cool plastic of the controller. His thumb hovers over the buttons, itching to push them.

"Prepare for a journey across the galaxy," the voice of the presenter echoes through the space, but Nico's attention is elsewhere. He presses a button, and suddenly the serene night sky above them pulses with life.

A beat drops, soft at first, then growing bolder—a tune that makes toes tap and heads bob. Lasers slice through the darkness, painting the cosmos with vibrant streaks of color. Comets dance to the rhythm, and planets spin as if they too feel the music. The classroom erupts into delighted gasps and laughter as children start dancing, the star show transformed into an interstellar concert.

"Whoa, is this supposed to happen?" a classmate whispers, pushing up his glasses.

"Science is amazing, huh?" Nico replies, a smirk playing on his lips as he revels in the secret of his own making.

For a moment, Nico is more than just a kid with a love for video games; he's a cosmic DJ orchestrating the heavens themselves.

"Best. Field trip. Ever," someone breathes out, and Nico nods, feeling like the luckiest kid in the world.

When the tour of the museum comes to an end, the bus rumbles and shakes as it heads back to school, the air is electric with excitement. Nico's classmates are still buzzing, their chatter a vibrant hum of amazement after the planetarium's unexpected light show.

"Did you see that? The stars were dancing!" one kid exclaims, throwing his hands up as if he could pluck a star from the sky.

"Totally epic," another agrees, voice filled with wonder.

Nico, sitting in his seat with a grin plastered across his face, soaks in the praise like a sponge. He doesn't say much; he doesn't need to. His handy work with the controller spoke volumes, and now he's basking in the glow of accomplishment.

As the bus turns a corner, the movement jostles Nico from his reverie. That's when he remembers—the controller. It should be safely tucked away in his backpack. Fumbling, he unzips the front pocket, the one where he stashed his precious gadget. But his hand meets only fabric and crumbs from a hastily packed lunch.

"Lucas," Nico says, urgency creeping into his voice as he turns to his friend, "do you have my controller?"

Lucas looks up from the window, his gaze flat, unperturbed by the sudden spike in tension. "I don't have it," he replies, shrugging nonchalantly.

Nico's heart skips a beat. Not good. He swivels around, eyes landing on Emma, who's humming a tune from the star show.

"Emma, do you—?"

She cuts him off with a soft chuckle. "Why would I have it? You boys never let me touch that thing."

There it is—a sinking feeling in the pit of Nico's stomach, like he's falling through space without a safety net. Panic flares up, hot and swift, but he forces a smile for Emma's sake. "Right, of course," he says, trying to laugh it off.

But inside, Nico's mind races. Where could the controller be?

Nico checks his bag once more, practically dumping it upside down onto the vinyl bus seat. It's definitely not there. His face pales, a ghostly white that seems at odds with the colorful buzz of his classmates chattering about the day's adventures. Nico's heart pounds and his eyes begin to well up.

"Think, Nico, think!" he mutters under his breath. Fighting back tears, he retraces his steps in his mind. Did he leave it in the planetarium? Near the T-Rex skeleton? The restroom? Each possibility feels more daunting than the last.

From the seat across the aisle, Lucas watches Nico's distress with a veiled smugness. A tight smile plays on his lips, but he's careful not to let anyone see. He leans back against the cushioned seat, arms crossed, feeling a peculiar satisfaction in watching Nico squirm. The controller had always been Nico's ticket to admiration, and Lucas couldn't help but feel a pang of envy every time Nico showed off.

"What's wrong, Nico? Lost something?" Lucas asks, feigning concern.

Nico nods, too anxious to speak. He feels like he's swallowed a block of ice, cold dread settling in his stomach. That controller isn't just a toy—it's part of who he is, an extension of his adventurous spirit.

Lucas, meanwhile, can't quite shake off a pesky sense of guilt that nags at him. It's one thing to wish for some of the limelight, quite another to see your friend in such a state. But then again, he reminds himself, Nico was always the one to get noticed, to be the hero of every schoolyard tale. Maybe it's only fair that someone else gets a turn, even if it's due to an unfortunate mishap.

"Too much attention isn't always good, you know," Lucas says, attempting to sound wise beyond his years. "Sometimes, laying low is better."

Nico doesn't seem to hear him; his thoughts far away, probably imagining the worst-case scenarios. But deep down, Lucas knows the truth—he misses the way things were before the controller came into their lives, when friendship was simpler and not overshadowed by envious whispers or the glare of the spotlight.

In that small bus filled with the excited voices of fifth graders, two boys sit wrapped in their own thoughts, each grappling with the weight of what it means to truly be a friend.

The science museum, with all its wonders and his precious controller, is retreating further into the distance with every second. Nico's fidgety hands betray a mind racing faster than the bus, thoughts tumbling over each other like sneakers in a dryer.

"Can't believe it's almost an hour away," he mutters to himself, picturing the controller lying somewhere cold and forgotten amongst dinosaur bones and spaceship models. Or worse, in the hands of someone else.

The bus squeaks to a stop, and the children pour out, all except Nico, who trails behind. He shuffles up to his teacher, who is gathering her things.

"Miss Jenkin?" he starts tentatively, nervously rocking back and forth. "Do you think there's a lost and found at the museum?"

She turns, a smile softening the lines on her face. "I'm sure there is, Nico. Museums always have a spot for misplaced treasures."

She tilts her head, sensing the importance of what's unsaid.

Nico's stomach does a backflip. This is it. He has to ask, but how can he explain the unexplainable?

"Can you, um, call and ask them to look around? For something I might've left?" he asks, his voice no more than a whisper caught in a breeze.

"Of course." Miss Jenkin nods, pulling out her phone. Then she pauses, eyes locking onto Nico's ocean blue ones. "What was it that you think you left at the museum?"

The question hangs heavy in the air, and Nico feels his cheeks flush. He opens his mouth, but words scurry away like mice from a cat. How can he tell her about the controller, the one thing that turned an ordinary field trip into an epic adventure?

His secret happiness, now a source of pure panic.

"Uh, it's..." Nico stammers, then swallows the lump forming in his throat.

Miss Jenkin waits patiently, her gaze kind but expectant. Nico knows he can't reveal the truth, not here, not now. His secret must stay hidden just a little longer, even if it twists his insides into knots.

"Never mind," he manages to say, his voice a little stronger, fueled by a hopeful idea blossoming in his mind.

"Okay, Nico. If you remember later, let me know," Miss Jenkin says, her voice trailing off as she gives him a gentle pat on the shoulder, oblivious to the storm raging inside her student.

As Nico walks away, the weight of his secret presses down, but a spark of resolve lights his path forward. He'll find a way to get the controller back, somehow, someway. It's an adventure waiting to happen, and Nico Carmichael never backs down from a challenge.

He collapses into his chair with a sigh that seems to carry all of yesterday's fun and today's trouble. His backpack slumps next to his desk like a guilty accomplice. Emma peeks at him from across the aisle, brimming with the same concern that always makes her seem wiser than her age.

"Did she call the museum?" Emma whispers, leaning closer.

Nico shakes his head, his fingers drumming an anxious rhythm on the wooden surface. "I couldn't do it. I just...you know?"

Emma tilts her head, urging him to go on with a look that could unlock secrets.

"I couldn't tell the teacher that I brought my controller to school, let alone the museum!"

Nico confesses in a hushed tone, as if the words are delicate creatures afraid of the light. "I'll have to call the museum myself when I get home."

"Are you going to be okay?" Emma's voice is soft but steady, like the gentle hand of a friend ready to catch you if you fall.

"Yeah." Nico nods, though his insides are still doing somersaults. "Yeah, I'll figure it out."

In the midst of his turmoil, there's a glimmer of hope. Maybe, just maybe, he can solve this puzzle himself without getting into a heap of trouble. After all, isn't that what every intrepid hero in his video games does? Face the big boss, save the day, and live to play another level.

With a deep breath, Nico lets the bell's shrill ring signal the end of another school day and the start of his next great mission: Operation Controller Retrieval.

At the sound of the school bell, Nico's sneakers slap against the pavement as he bolts through the school's front double doors. Once home, he flings his backpack onto the kitchen table, the contents spilling out like candy from a piñata. His fingers dance across the keyboard of the family computer, eyes scanning the screen for the number that might reunite him with his precious controller.

"Come on, come on," he mutters under his breath, the cursor finally landing on the phone number he's been seeking. The digits blur together as he punches them into the home phone, holding his breath with every beep of the dial tone.

Ring... ring... Silence hangs in the air, heavy and unwelcome. With each unanswered call, his hopes deflate a little more. He glances at the clock, biting his lip; it's nearly closing time.

"Maybe everyone went home early..." he whispers to himself, trying to ward off the disappointment. But Nico isn't one to give up—after all, every quest has its hurdles, and this is just another level to beat.

Giving it one last shot, he redials the number, the sound echoing in the quiet house. This time, the ringing stops abruptly, replaced by sudden voice.

"Science Museum, front desk. How can I help you?" The voice is brusque but welcoming, like the bark of a friendly dog.

"Hi! I was at the museum earlier today, and I think I might've left something really important there," Nico rushes out, his words tumbling over each other. He can almost see the end of the level, the controller gleaming just beyond reach.

"Can you hold on for a moment?" the voice asks, and Nico nods before realizing the man can't see him. "Sure thing," he says instead, gripping the phone so tightly his knuckles turn white.

"Thanks for waiting. We're about to close up, but if you tell me what it is, I'll leave a note for someone to check tomorrow morning," the man says upon returning to the line.

"Gosh, sir. It's really important," Nico insists. "Would you mind checking now?"

The voice at the other end rumbled, then said, "Fine. Tell me what you left."

Nico's heart does a victory lap in his chest. It's not game over yet.

"Okay, it's a game controller, about yay big," Nico starts, stretching his hands to describe the size of the controller in the air, as if the front desk man could see him. "It's black with blue and red buttons." He giggles nervously, knowing full well it does more than look cool.

"I thought you said you left something important?" the man at the desk says.

"It is important. It's really important to me," Nico justifies.

"Well, son, you're in luck," the man's voice crackling through the phone with a hint of surprise.

"Someone just turned in a controller that matches your description. Got it an hour ago. Why would anyone bring this thing to a museum?" The man asked rhetorically.

Nico's heart leaps. A grin spreads across his face, so wide it threatens to split his face in two. "That's it! That's my controller!"

"Great to hear, kid. So, where do you want me to send it?" The man's question is routine, expected, but it throws Nico for a loop.

"Oh, uh, can you hold on a sec?" Nico stammers. His mind races. He can't break Mom's number one rule: Never give out your personal information to strangers. Not even if it means getting back the coolest thing he's ever owned.

"Sure, I'll wait," the man replies, a hint of impatience seeping into his tone.

Nico bites his lip, pondering his next move. He needs that controller, but there's no way he's going to slip up on safety. Not today, not ever.

Nico's fingers tap a frantic rhythm on the kitchen counter, each beat another reminder of the pickle he's in. He chews on his lower lip, eyes darting around as if the answer might be scribbled on the fridge or hiding in the fruit bowl. His mom's voice hums from her office, a steady stream of big work words that mean Not Now, Nico.

"What am I going to do? I can't give out my address?" he mutters under his breath, heart thudding against his ribs like it wants to escape and solve the problem itself. His controller is so close, yet worlds away without a safe path back to him.

"Son, are you going to give me your address or not?" The man's voice crackles through the phone, pushing Nico back to the task at hand. The man sounds like he has no time for games, even though a game controller is precisely the subject of their call.

Nico grips the phone tighter, the plastic creaking a silent plea for patience. He feels the heat rise to his cheeks, because here he is, stuck between the rock-solid rule of personal safety and the hard place of his beloved controller being who-knows-where.

"Um, just a minute longer, please," Nico stalls, buying time he doesn't have. He wishes for a pause button in real life, something to freeze the moment while he figures out a winning strategy. But life doesn't come with cheat codes, and Nico knows he'll have to level up on his own this time.

Nico's thumb hovers over the end call button as the seconds tick away. If he could, he'd hit fast-forward on life, zip through this uncomfortable moment, and land in a future where his controller is back in his hands. But time isn't a video game, and Nico can't skip levels.

"Sorry, may I call you back?" he blurts out, voice high-pitched with worry. His eyes dart around the room, scanning for an out—a lifeline, anything.

The man on the other line lets out a sigh that travels down the phone line and into Nico's ear like a gust of wind ready to blow away his chances. "I clock out in 5 minutes," the man says, sharp and to the point.

He might as well have said 'Game Over' because that's what it feels like to Nico—an adventure stalling out, the final countdown kicking in. Nico's mind races faster than his heart, he needs a power-up, a boost, something to push him past the finish line.

But all he has is his wits, his will, and a ticking clock reminding him that sometimes, life's puzzles don't come with instructions.

"OK, I'll hurry," Nico says, pressing the red button on the screen with a sense of urgency that makes his finger tremble. He swivels around in his chair, dialing the number for his best friend. When he hears Lucas on the other end, before his friend could even say hello, Nico asks for his help.

"Lucas," Nico starts, words tumbling out in a rush, "I need a huge favor." He leans over, hands clasped together as if he's about to unveil a secret level in one of his video games.

Lucas lowers the comic, one eyebrow arching up like the beginning of a challenging game stage. "What's up?" he asks, his tone casual, but his eyes, sharp as arrow tips, miss nothing.

"Can I use your address?" Nico blurts out. The thought of his controller drifting in limbo, possibly snagged by another kid with sticky fingers, sends a shiver down his spine. "The museum guy, he found my controller and he can send it back, but I can't give him my home address without Mom's permission and she's on a work call."

Lucas' eyes flicker with surprise, then a calculating glint takes over. He pauses for a moment that stretches too long for Nico's comfort, before breaking into a slow smile. "Sure, you can use my address," Lucas replies, the words sliding out smooth. "My mom will be fine with it." He says without actually asking him mom for approval.

Relief washes over Nico like the feeling of hitting save on his progress before the final boss battle. He bounces on his heels, a grin stretching across his face, bright as the glow from a treasure chest opening. "You're a lifesaver, Lucas! And an amazing friend" he says, the muscles in his shoulders relaxing as if a great weight has been lifted.

Nico chirps with a mix of gratitude and urgency, his fingers already flying over the phone's keypad. He punches in the numbers faster than he clears levels in his favorite video game. The line rings once, twice, then—

"Hello? Science Museum front desk," a voice answers, tinged with the sound of someone who's had a long day.

"Hi again! It's me, Nico Carmichael. I called about my controller?" Nico's words tumble out in a hurried stream. "I've got an address for you to send it to."

"Go ahead," the man replies, the sound of rustling papers echoing through the receiver as he presumably prepares to jot down the details.

Nico rattles off Lucas's address, each number an anchor pulling his worries back to shore. The man repeats it back, confirming the information, and Nico nods even though he knows the man can't see.

"Got it. We'll ship it out as soon as possible," the museum employee confirms.

"Thank you so much!" Nico says, the relief in his voice evident.

Leaning back in his chair, a contented sigh escapes him. The weight of worry that had been pressing on his chest like a stack of textbooks lifts, and he feels light, almost buoyant. Today is the day he learns that sometimes, losing control isn't the end of the world. Sometimes, it's just another puzzle to solve.

CHAPTER 8
Friendship vs. Jealousy

A few days later, Lucas rips open the package on his front porch with a grin so wide it could split his face. The controller, with its sleek buttons and shiny surface, sits in his hands like a treasure chest of endless possibilities. He doesn't rush to tell Nico; instead, he pockets the device, feeling its weight against his thigh as he plots.

"Hey, Lucas," Nico calls out during lunch recess, bounding up to him with that familiar spark of hope in his eyes. "Did the controller come yet?" He gives Lucas an expectant look, hopeful that he will have his precious controller in his hands once again.

Lucas shakes his head, hiding the truth behind a casual shrug. "No, not yet. Maybe the mail's slow this week." He watches

Nico's face fall, just a little, and feels a twinge of something he can't quite name.

"Man, I've been checking my YouTube channel every day, imagining all the new tricks we could show off," Nico says, his voice tinged with disappointment. But he quickly bounces back, a smile plastered on his face as if to say he's okay with waiting. Just a bit longer.

"Sure, sure, it'll be epic," Lucas agrees with feigned enthusiasm, turning away to hide the coy glint in his expression. He knows Nico trusts him, but trust is a game piece in Lucas's strategic mind.

Day after day, Nico asks, and day after day, Lucas tells the same lie. With each question, Nico's shoulders droop a fraction more, his enthusiasm dims like a flickering lightbulb. Yet, he remains oblivious to the deceit, his spirit undeterred, believing in a friendship that Lucas has already gambled away.

Lucas tucks his hands into his pockets as he strolls out to the playground, Emma at his side. They sidestep a game of hopscotch, exchanging a quick, secretive look before they head toward the monkey bars, away from Nico. Their voices are hushed, their heads bent together in a bubble of conspiracy.

"Okay, so we have it," Lucas starts, glancing over his shoulder to make sure Nico isn't within earshot. "But how do we get him to do what we want without making it obvious?"

Emma frowns, her curls bouncing as she shakes her head. "I don't like this, Lucas. It doesn't feel right."

"Come on, Emma," Lucas coaxes with a sly smile. "Think of it as... a test of his friendship. We're not making him do anything; we're just seeing what he's willing to do for us."

Emma bites her lower lip, looking unconvinced but slowly nodding. She's always trying to see the good in people, even when Lucas is steering things down a darker path.

"Fine," she relents, though she is obviously uneasy. "But only to see if he really is a good friend, right?."

"Exactly," Lucas agrees, a note of triumph in his voice.

Meanwhile, Nico stands alone by the swings, kicking at the pebbles with his worn sneakers, much different from the expensive ones he could manifest with the controller. He watches other kids play, laughter and shouts fill the air around him, but there's no invitation for him to join. The controller that once put him in the spotlight now casts a shadow, keeping him on the outskirts.

"Lucas said it didn't come yet," he mumbles to himself. But part of him wonders why his friends are suddenly so distant, whispering to each other and leaving him out. They used to share everything, every level-up, every high score, every recess plan. Now, it seems like there's a level he can't reach, a game he can't play.

Unbeknownst to Nico, Lucas is already plotting the next move. His mind races with possibilities, eager to exploit Nico's eagerness and test the boundaries of their fraying friendship. If only Nico would realize that sometimes, the game changes and the rules aren't what they seem.

Nico's heart sinks as he watches Emma and Lucas huddled together by the monkey bars, their heads nearly touching as they share secrets, he's not a part of. He shuffles his feet, the weight of exclusion make him feel small and insignificant. His gaze follows them, tracing the path of their laughter that seems to bounce off the playground equipment and float away from him, unreachable.

The void where the controller used to be is like an invisible wall between Nico and his friends. He can almost hear the questions piling up from other kids, wondering why he's not doing those cool tricks anymore, the ones that made jaws drop and eyes pop only weeks before.

"Hey Nico!" a voice calls out, and for a second his heart leaps. Maybe it's an invitation back into the fold. But the hope deflates just as quickly when he turns to see a group of classmates, their curiosity plain on their faces. "Do that thing where you make the ball hover!"

His fingers twitch, instinctively reaching for something that isn't there. There's no use pretending. With a small sigh, Nico shakes his head, a tinge of red creeping up his cheeks. "I... I can't."

"Come on, man! You were so good at it," another chimes in, but Nico only shrugs, feeling smaller with each passing second. It's tough, this explaining business. Without the controller, his tricks are just regular, the kind anyone could do with enough practice. And practice is something he hasn't been doing much of lately. His ordinary skills don't stand up to the memory of controller-enhanced spectacles.

"Sorry, guys," he says with a forced smile. Nico can feel the letdown, and his heart stumbles.

Nico turns away, his eyes stinging, fighting back tears, he takes a deep breath. He remembers how it felt to be extraordinary, to be the one everyone watched with wide-eyed wonder. But that was then, and this is now—a now where he has to find his footing without the magic of a controller. As he walks towards the edge of the playground, he reminds himself that he's still Nico Carmichael, still a passionate gamer with an active YouTube channel and a knack for making the best out of any game he plays.

"Got to level up the hard way, I guess," he mutters, determination lighting a spark in his eyes. Today might not be his day, but tomorrow is unwritten.

After a lonely recess is over, Nico shuffles back into class, his sneakers scuffing with every step. Gone are the flashy kicks that made him feel powerful, cool, and extraordinary. He tugs at the sleeve of his plain blue hoodie—the kind you could pick up at any department store on sale—and tries not to think about the designer gear he used to flaunt.

"Hey, Nico." Emma waves from her desk, her smile genuine but tinged with concern. Lucas, sitting beside her, doesn't even glance up from his notebook, scribbling away at some devious plan or another.

"Hi, Emma," Nico replies, mustering a half-hearted wave back as he slips into his seat just as the bell rings.

Miss Jenkin starts the lesson, but whispers bubble around the room. Nico catches snippets, words like "ordinary" and "boring" that seem to stick to him like gum on his shoe. He frowns, glancing around to see fewer eyes on him than usual. The gaggle of classmates who once jockeyed for a spot near him now cluster around other kids, the ones with the latest gadgets and trendiest clothes.

"Did you see Marco's new watch?" one girl gushes to her friend, pointing across the room where Marco is showing off the newest Apple watch.

"Yeah, it's so cool! It's got like, a million features!" the other responds, both of them giggling as they admire it from afar.

Nico feels an invisible weight settling on his shoulders, heavy and uncomfortable. He used to be the one with the cool stuff, the one everyone wanted to hang out with. But now, without the controller's magic touch, he's just... well, just Nico. His fingers itch for the familiar feel of a gamepad, for the digital world where he knows he can still be a hero. But here, in the real world, it's a different story.

Back at home after the long day, Alfie's cheerful voice cuts through Nico's sad thoughts. The little guy is already dribbling a ball with impressive skill for a five-year-old. "Hey, Nico, wanna play soccer?"

"Maybe later, Alf," Nico says, forcing a smile for his brother's sake. "You go on ahead." Alfie shrugs and dashes off, joining a group of neighborhood kids eager to include the energetic boy in their game.

"Psst, Nico," Piper sidles up to him, her green eyes sharp with sisterly insight. "You okay?"

"Sure, I'm fine," he lies, because what else can he say? That he misses being the center of attention? That he wishes things were as easy as pressing a button?

"Okay, if you say so," she replies, not entirely convinced but letting it slide as she skips off to do some dancing on the grass.

Nico watches her go, sees the ease with which she moves between groups, making friends without the need for anything but her sunny personality and curiosity. Maybe, he thinks, there's something to learn from that. Maybe there's more to life than being extraordinary in ways that only last until the next big thing comes along.

He takes a deep breath, feeling the crisp air fill his lungs. It's time to stop worrying about what he's lost and start appreciating what he still has—a family that loves him, a brain full of ideas, and a whole lot of video games waiting for him upstairs in his room. With a nod to himself, Nico decides it's high time to level up the old-fashioned way: through hard work, resilience, and maybe, just maybe, a bit of everyday magic.

On his bed, Nico hunches over his notebook, the tip of his pencil jabbing at the paper as he sketches out a new level design for his favorite video game. His brow is furrowed, concentration etching deep lines in his young face. He's not just doodling to pass the time; he's on a mission. No magical controller means no shortcuts, and he's determined to prove he can be a whiz kid without any tricks up his sleeve.

He rubs his eyes, weary but not defeated. His fingers are smudged with pencil lead, a badge of honor. The figures on the page start to take shape: intricate platforms, tricky obstacles, and hidden rewards. It's all there, a world born from his imagination.

"Looks tough," Emma says, plopping down beside him. Her hair tumbles over her shoulders, catching the last rays of sunlight. "Think you can do it?"

"Absolutely," Nico responds, the hint of a smile playing on his lips. It's not bravado speaking—it's belief. In this moment, he knows that every failed jump, every restart, every extra hour poured into perfecting his craft is just part of the journey. A journey back to himself.

"Let me know if you need a beta tester," Emma offers, nudging his shoulder with her own.

"Will do," he nods, grateful for her unwavering support.

"Remember, practice makes perfect!" Piper calls out to him.

"Practice and then some," Nico mutters under his breath. He knows now that the truest form of magic doesn't come from a controller; it comes from within, from the heart, and from the persistence to keep trying, no matter how ordinary the starting point might seem.

CHAPTER 9
Making Things Right

The sun dapples through the leaves of the old oak tree, as Nico Carmichael fidgets with an imaginary game controller, buried in thought. He can't shake the image of Lucas and Emma from his mind, their laughter echoing like a tune he can't reset.

"Jealousy is a glitch in friendship," he mumbles to a carefree ant he notices in the dirt. The empty space where Lucas and Emma sit next to him, feels cold and unfriendly.

With a heavy sigh, Nico stands up, dusts off his jeans, and wanders into his cluttered garage, dodging a minefield of skateboards and garden tools. He spots the old, rusty lockbox that once held his father's prized baseball cards. A lightbulb flickers on in his brain.

"Once I find that controller," he declares to a box of Christmas decorations, "I'm locking it up in here." The idea solidifies like the final piece of a puzzle clicking into place. No more tempting fate with that thing. If locking it away means getting his friends back, then that's the play he's willing to make.

The lockbox feels heavy in his hands, symbolizing the weight of his decision. Nico can't help but hope that this is what it takes to mend the fraying edges of his friendships.

"Now," he tells a curious squirrel that's paused to look up at him, "I've got to find that controller." The squirrel, unimpressed by human dilemmas, scampers off, leaving Nico to ponder his next move alone.

Echoes of playful chaos that is the park on a sunny afternoon, call in the distance. Nico decides to go for a bike ride to clear his mind. The wind sweeping through his messy blonde hair as if trying to untangle his thoughts, Nico sees the park come into view. Green and inviting with its sprawling fields and towering oaks whispering secrets to each other, Nico's heart pangs for a moment. Kids are laughing, their voices mingling with the twittering of birds and the rustle of leaves, and he can't help but miss those afternoons spent here with his buddies. He hasn't gamed in days, and it feels like an eternity has been crammed into each minute without the familiar glow of his console.

Nico is oblivious to the fact that his trusty controller—the one that fit in his hands better than any other, the one with his own name labeled on the back —isn't lost or misplaced. It's not buried under a pile of comic books or nestled between couch cushions. Instead, it's right under his nose, sitting comfortably in the hands of Lucas and Emma. But Nico doesn't suspect a thing. He's too wrapped up in the idea of rekindling friendships gone awry.

Coasting to a stop at the bike rack, Nico expertly hops off as the wheels spin their last revolution. He locks his bike up, the chain snaking around the frame and through the tire, securing it with a satisfying click. With his hands now free, he shoves them into his pockets and heads toward the familiar bench where they used to gather.

"Maybe it's just been a glitch," he murmurs to himself, scanning the park for a sign of normalcy, for a hint that things could go back to the way they were before scores and screens got in the way.

But there's no reset button for friendship, and as he strides across the grass, he knows that finding the controller won't fix everything. Yet, with each step, he's determined to try—to find that missing link and lock it away if it means he might laugh with Lucas and Emma again without the shadow of jealousy looming over them.

As he nears his favorite spot, he slows down, a familiar sound nudging his curiosity like a persistent itch. That's when he spots them: Lucas and Emma, tossing something gleefully between them.

Nico squints as he recognizes the object mid-flight. It couldn't be. But it is—it's the controller! His heart does a strange little flip, caught between betrayal and an odd sense of relief. Without missing a beat, the controller arcs through the air, passing from Lucas's outstretched hand to Emma's, her curls bouncing with each movement.

"Hey, watch it!" Lucas barks with a laugh, as Emma nearly fumbles the catch. Their carefree chuckles ripple through the air, a stark contrast to the tightness in Nico's chest.

For a moment, Nico considers clearing his throat, stepping forward, demanding answers. But something holds him back—a whisper of wisdom that tells him this isn't the battle to pick. Not now. Maybe not ever.

So, instead of confronting them, he simply watches from a distance, an invisible spectator to this scene. A sigh slips from his lips, and with a slight shake of his head, he decides to retreat. Nico turns around, the thoughts swirling in his head now quieter, almost hushed. He's actually relieved, in a way that surprises him. The weight of the mystery that had been pressing on his shoulders feels lighter now, even if the confusion remains.

The journey home is different; there's no rush, no urgency. It's just Nico, his bike, and the open road, stretching out like the beginning of a new chapter—one where controllers and high scores don't dictate the plot twists and turns.

He realizes that friendship isn't about who holds the power or who comes out on top. It's about the moments you share, the laughter that bubbles up unexpectedly, and the quiet understanding that sometimes, things change. And maybe, just maybe, that's okay.

Nico pedals steadily, considering that the piece of plastic holds no real power unless it's in his hands, and yet it's caused such a rift. His grip on the handlebars tightens for a moment. Winning virtual battles is thrilling, but it's nothing compared to the adventures he's had with his friends. It's them he misses—Lucas's goofy grin, Emma's quick wit.

As he turns into his driveway, he sees Piper and Alfie drawing with chalk.

"Hey, Nico!" Piper's voice pulls him from his reverie. She's got that look in her green eyes, the one that says she's cooked up some new scheme to conquer boredom.

"Hey, Pipes," he calls back, a genuine smile tugging at his lips. He drops his bike by the porch, the kickstand scraping against the walkway.

"Whatcha thinking about?" she asks, tilting her head like she can peer straight into his mind.

"Stuff," he replies, which isn't exactly a lie. It's just not the entire truth either.

"Want to hang out?" Piper's hopeful gaze meets his, and he feels a tug in his chest. The controller, the games—they seem so far away now. His main concern shouldn't be a missing gadget; it should be mending fences, rebuilding bridges.

"Sure, let's stay outside," Nico decides and follows Piper to their backyard. They end up sprawled on the grass, watching clouds drift lazily across the sky, each one a blank canvas for their imagination. Piper points out shapes, and Nico finds himself laughing, really laughing, for the first time in days.

"Looks like a dragon," he points upwards, "breathing fire."

"Or a knight with a shield!" Piper counters, her enthusiasm infectious.

"Maybe both," Nico concedes with a grin, rolling onto his side to face her.

Sometimes, he thinks, you don't need a controller to embark on an adventure or to create a world worth exploring. Sometimes, all it takes is a patch of grass, a clear sky, and someone who understands that the best stories are the ones you make up as you go along.

Nico kicks a pebble across the yard, watching it skitter into the base of the old shed. The wooden door creaks as he pries it open, sunlight slicing through the dust motes that dance in the air. He spots the blue handle of an old tennis racquet poking out from behind a stack of gardening tools.

"Hey, Piper, look what I found!" He hoists two mismatched racquets into the light, their strings still taut enough for some backyard fun.

Piper claps her hands, her eyes lighting up like fireworks. "Awesome! And I've got the ping pong balls!" she exclaims, rummaging through an old cardboard box and emerging with a triumphant grin.

In no time, they set up their makeshift court. With each volley, the ping pong ball zips back and forth, creating a rhythm that echoes in the laughter bouncing between them. Nico lunges for a particularly crafty shot by Piper, just barely tapping the ball over their imagined net, an old clothesline strung low to the ground.

Piper chases after it, her feet thudding against the soft earth. "I love playing with you, Nico!" she says, her voice bubbling over with joy as she sends the ball spinning back his way.

Nico can't help but smile, the corners of his eyes crinkling. His heart feels lighter, like it's been lifted on the breeze that rustles through the leaves above them. "I really enjoy spending time with you too, Pipes," he replies, swatting the ball back gently so she can reach it.

The game continues, easy and carefree, as shadows begin to lengthen across the lawn. Nico finds himself lost in the moment, the weight of worries about friendships and controllers slipping away with each playful rally.

A golden sunset casts a warm glow over the backyard as Nico and Piper chase the ping pong ball, their laughter mingling with the chirping of crickets. The air is filled with the scent of freshly cut grass, and in this little slice of paradise, they're champions of their own making.

Piper's eyes sparkle as she returns Nico's serve, her curly hair bouncing with each move. "No way!" Piper exclaims when Nico makes a particularly impressive save, panting lightly from the exertion.

As the game winds down, Nico gathers the scattered ping pong balls while Piper flops onto the grass in exhaustion. He sits beside her, the cool blades tickling his skin, and takes a deep breath. It's time for a heart-to-heart with his sister.

"Hey, Pipes," Nico starts, his voice softer now. "There's something I have to tell you." He fiddles with a ping pong ball, rolling it between his palms. "It's about the controller..." His words trail off for a moment as he looks into her attentive gaze.

Piper sits up, her expression serious but supportive. "What about it?" she prompts gently, brushing a strand of hair from her face.

He hesitates, then dives in. "Well, it's kind of the reason I've been so caught up in my thoughts lately." Nico confesses, choosing his words carefully. "And... it's gone missing."

Piper's mouth forms an 'o' of surprise. "Missing? How?"

Nico shrugs, feeling a mix of confusion and relief. But then, he decides to tell Piper the whole story. Starting with the man at the front desk of the museum asking for an address to send the controller, then the difficulties of trying to be cool among his classmates and then describing how terrible it felt to see his friends playing without him.

Piper reaches out, giving his hand a reassuring squeeze. "Hey, it's going to be okay. You're so smart, Nico. I know you'll figure it out," she assures him, warmth radiating from her voice. Nico nods, grateful for her support.

The sincerity in her voice wraps around Nico like a warm blanket. She beams at him, her eyes shining with that little-sister brand of respect. "Thanks for telling me, Nico," she says, scooting closer to wrap an arm around his shoulders. Then she stands up quickly and playfully asks, "How about one more game before Mom calls us in?"

"You're on!" Nico says, picking up his racquet ready to win. He twirls the old tennis racquet in his hand, the mesh whispering as it slices through the air. Piper scoops up another ping pong ball and tosses it to him, her eyes narrowed in concentration. He's about to swing when she holds up a hand, pausing their game.

"Hey, Nico," Piper says, biting her lip thoughtfully. "Have you thought about talking to Lucas and Emma about the controller? Maybe there's been some kind of mix-up. A misunderstanding, perhaps?"

Nico freezes, the racquet hanging limply by his side now. The idea of confronting them tugs at his nerves, but there's a ring of truth to Piper's suggestion. His friends might have their reasons, and he can't help but feel a glimmer of hope that this is all just one big misunderstanding.

"Yeah, I guess," Nico admits, scuffing his sneaker on the ground. "Maybe they didn't mean to keep it from me." His heart thumps unevenly, half out of fear, half out of an eagerness to smooth things over.

"Exactly!" Piper exclaims, clapping her hands together. "You won't know until you ask, right?"

"Right," he echoes, nodding more firmly this time. Deep down, Nico knows that talking to Lucas and Emma is the right thing to do. It's what heroes in his favorite games always do—they face their problems head-on, even when it's scary.

"Okay, I'll talk to them," he decides, lifting his chin with newfound resolve. "I want to hear their side of the story."

"Good for you, Nico!" Piper cheers, her encouragement ringing in his ears like the victory music from his favorite video game level. With a determined breath, Nico sets down the racquet and prepares for a different kind of challenge—the kind that doesn't come with a reset button.

CHAPTER 10
Friendship Unraveling

The stolen controller weighs heavy on Nico's mind, and he can't shake off the uneasy feeling bubbling up inside him. He sits on his front porch, waiting for Lucas and Emma. When he sees the two step off the sidewalk, Nico jumps up.

"Lucas," Nico starts when, his voice sharper than usual, "we need to talk about the controller." Emma's hazel eyes flicker between the two boys, sensing the tension as it thickens the air. She chews on her lip, wishing she could smooth things over before they unravel any further.

Lucas places one foot on the first step, his arms folded over his chest, an impish grin forming. "What about it?"

Nico pauses, his hands clenched into fists at his sides.

"I want it back," Nico says knowingly.

"Sure, you can have it back. But...you've gotta use it for something that is fun for all of us," Lucas finishes, tilting his head to one side as if he's just proposed the most reasonable deal in the world.

"More fun for everyone?" Nico repeats, wondering what that entails since he is the only one who holds the power. He glances at Emma, hoping for some understanding in her warm gaze, but she seems to be wrestling with her own thoughts.

"Exactly," Lucas replies, a triumphant edge creeping into his voice as he watches Nico squirm under the proposition.

"We are bored watching you have all the fun!" Lucas declares, breaking the tense silence that has fallen between them. His brown eyes fix on Nico with an intensity that feels like a challenge.

"Yeah, it's no fair," Emma chimes in, her curly red locks bouncing as she nods in agreement. Her hazel eyes, usually so warm and comforting, now hold a flash of frustration.

Nico swallows hard. He'd always thought video games were his way to shine, a chance to escape into a world where he could be the hero, the one everyone cheered for. But now, standing here under the judgmental stares of his two best friends, he realizes that maybe he's been hogging the spotlight. He hadn't realized how much his popularity had affected the friendship.

He looks from Lucas to Emma, their faces expectant, waiting for him to make a move. The controller was supposed to bring them together, not tear them apart. In his heart, Nico knows what friendship is about—

sharing adventures, not going solo while others watch from the sidelines.

"Okay, okay," he murmurs, trying to keep the tremble out of his voice. "Let's think of something we can all enjoy." He doesn't know how he'll manage it, but he's determined to find a way to mend the rift.

Nico kicks a small pebble across the schoolyard, his brows furrowed in thought. He's searching for a way to keep the peace, to make the fun fair and square for everyone. The chill in the air nips at his cheeks, but it's the coolness between the friends that really gives him shivers.

"Hey, I have an idea!" Lucas blurts out, breaking the uneasy silence with what appears to be enthusiasm, but he'd been plotting the idea for weeks. He points toward Mrs. Foster's house next door where they can see a stack of pumpkins perfectly placed to welcome neighbors. "Smash all those pumpkins with one shot. Just like you take out the bad guys in a battle!"

The suggestion sends a ripple of shock through Nico. He never imagined his own friend would turn the tables on him like this. Torn between the longing for approval from his friends and the unease at Lucas's proposal, Nico finds himself at a crossroads. What Lucas suggests doesn't sit right with him, and he knows it.

Emma giggles behind her hand, her eyes sparkling with mischief. Nico feels a knot form in his stomach. That doesn't sound like fun; it sounds mean.

"Or hey," Lucas continues, spotting a pile of recycling bins full of glass bottles on the end of the driveway, "Get the mail carrier to trip over those!"

These are not the adventures Nico had in mind when he first discovered the magic of the controller. He pictures Eddie, the mailman tumbling, his tote bag flying, face red with embarrassment, or worse, hurt. How could anyone find joy in that?

Lucas rattles off another suggestion, each one more cringe-worthy than the last. Emma is laughing now, a sound that once felt like music to Nico's ears but now just rings hollow. He looks towards his house, he can see Alfie and Piper playing inside through the window, oblivious to the brewing storm outside.

"Those aren't jokes, Lucas," Nico finally says, his voice firmer than he feels. "They're just...not kind." He watches the clouds drift lazily above, wishing he could be as free and unbothered as they are.

"Come on, Nico! It'll be hilarious!" Lucas insists, not catching the unease in Nico's eyes or the way his hands ball into fists at his sides. These weren't the games Nico loved, the ones filled with challenges and victories. This was real life, with real feelings, and the stakes felt too high for a laugh.

Nico knew one thing for sure: no game was worth losing friends over, especially not like this.

Nico's hands are still balled into fists, his knuckles turning as white as the drifting clouds above. His gaze shifts from Lucas to the ground, where a tiny ladybug steadily across a crack in the pavement. He imagines what it must be like to carry on, undisturbed by the chaos of others' making.

"Lucas, I can't do that stuff," Nico says, shaking his head. "It's just mean."

Lucas' face turns a shade darker, eyes narrowing into slits. "What are you, scared?" he taunts, stepping closer until he's towering over Nico. "We're supposed to have fun together!"

"Fun doesn't mean hurting other people," Nico counters. He remembers the laughs and cheers when he'd first shown them the magic tricks he could do with the controller, but this was a far cry from those days.

"Fine, be boring!" Lucas's voice rises, drawing the attention of some nearby children walking towards them. "You're not a superhero, Nico!" he shouts, the words echoing through Nico like icicles.

Nico's heart sinks, his stomach queasy as if he swallowed rotten eggs. The controller in his pocket feels like it's burning a hole through his jeans, a reminder of the power he holds and the choices he has to make.

Lucas storms off, his shoes kicking up tiny puffs of dust with each step. His face is still red from arguing with Nico, and he's not done yet—not by a long shot. He zeroes in on the group of kids on the sidewalk, their chatter pausing as Lucas approaches.

"Hey, guys!" Lucas calls out, forcing a smile that doesn't reach his eyes. "You know Nico, right? Thinks he can do whatever he wants because he's got some... special tricks."

The kids exchange glances, curiosity piqued. They remember Nico's amazing feats, how he made things move without touching them, and the day he somehow managed to speed up the swing set like it was turbo-charged. But now, Lucas is casting shadows of doubt over those memories.

"Look," Lucas continues, leaning in like he's sharing a secret, "he's just putting on a show. A selfish one! We could all be having fun, but no, Mr. Superpowers chooses to be a total downer." The word 'superpowers' hangs in the air, heavy with sarcasm.

Emma stands off to the side, fidgeting with the hem of her shirt. She watches uneasily as the crowd begins to nod along with Lucas. It doesn't feel right, what he's doing, but she's caught in the middle. Her loyalty to Nico wars with her desire to keep the peace.

"Let's just ignore him," Lucas suggests, his voice dripping with faux concern. "We don't need his magic tricks to have a good time. Right?"

A murmur of agreement ripples through the group. Kids look at each other, shrugging as if to say, "Why not?" They've been swayed by Lucas's words, not fully understanding the magic controller's true nature or the weight that rests on Nico's shoulders.

Meanwhile, Nico stands alone on his porch, his gaze fixed on the ground. He's aware of Lucas's campaign against him, even from a distance. His fingers twitch, tempted to use the controller to set things right, but he resists. This isn't a game, and he won't become what Lucas accuses him of being. Instead, he takes a deep breath and lifts his head, determined to face this challenge without shortcuts—like a real hero would.

Lucas keeps talking as he watches more kids gather around him. He loved all the attention. So, this is what it felt like, Lucas thought. "You know," Lucas starts, his voice casual but loud enough for everyone to hear, "Nico isn't as cool as you think." A few kids snicker, casting sideways glances at Nico.

Nico feels a hot tear stream down his cheek as he listens to what Lucas says next.

"Seriously, guys," Lucas continues, pushing off the wall and stepping into the circle of classmates. "All that stuff? It's just lame tricks. Anyone could do it if they wanted." His words carry a sting, and some of the kids nod as if they've been thinking the same thing all along.

Nico's heart sinks. He clenches his fists, the hurt evident. He wants to speak up, to defend himself, but the words get stuck in his throat. Instead, he swallows hard, feeling the weight of their stares. He's always been the one to figure things out, to push boundaries and share his findings on his YouTube channel. But now, standing there under the harsh judgment of his peers, his confidence falters. He doesn't say anything. He turns and walks into his house, closing the front door on the group of kids still gathered outside.

That night, Nico lies in bed, staring at the ceiling. The echo of Lucas's words and the laughter of his classmates play over and over in his mind. He tries to get comfortable, squeezing his eyes shut in hopes of blocking out the memory of the day. But it's no use. The sense of betrayal cuts deep.

In the morning, Nico's alarm blares, but he doesn't move to turn it off. Instead, he musters the most pitiful cough he can and calls out weakly, "Mom, I don't feel so good." He hears footsteps approaching and closes his eyes, feigning sleep. When his mom peeks in, he pretends to stir awake, putting on a show of being ill.

Mrs. Carmichael strokes his hair, pushing the blonde strands back from his forehead. She knows Nico is not physically sick, but perhaps feels unwell in another way making it hard to get out of bed. "You're really going through something tough, huh? Let's call it a mental health day, okay?" she suggests, her voice the epitome of warmth. "I'll be working from home today, so if you need anything, I'm right downstairs."

Relief washes over Nico, a soothing balm to his frayed nerves. A mental health day. No expectations, no pressure to pretend everything's fine. Just time and space to breathe, to mend the cracks in his spirit.

"You're the best, Mom" he whispers, grateful for the understanding that hangs in the air between them, unspoken but deeply felt. He doesn't have to face school today, doesn't have to see the disappointment or the smirks. But as the house falls quiet and his mom begins her day downstairs, Nico can't shake the sadness that clings to him like a shadow.

He turns away from his video game console, the sight of it now bringing more pain than pleasure. Without his friends the games seem empty. He buries his face in his pillow, wishing for everything to go back to normal. If only everything could go back to the way it was before magic controllers and arguments about who has all the fun.

Nico's room is a fortress of solitude as the mid-morning sun peeks through the blinds, casting lines of light across his rumpled bedspread. His heart feels like a lump of clay—shapeless and heavy. He draws the covers up to his chin, trying to shield himself from the day that waits beyond his bedroom door.

Downstairs, Mrs. Carmichael taps on her laptop, pausing every so often to listen for sounds from above. She knows her son, the normally chipper boy with an adventurous streak, isn't himself today. With a mother's intuition, she senses the silent storm brewing in Nico's heart.

The clock ticks on, the house wrapped in an unusual hush. Mrs. Carmichael rises from her desk, making her way up the stairs with a determination softened by empathy. She raps gently on Nico's door before pushing it open. The sight of her boy, cocooned in blankets, eyes downcast and lost in thought, tugs at her heartstrings.

"Hey there," she begins, perching on the edge of Nico's bed. "How are you feeling?"

"Okay," he whispers, but truly unsure himself.

Mrs. Carmichael gives him a gentle squeeze on the shoulder, her touch light but filled with a mother's love. She leans against the doorframe, her eyes soft and full of empathy. "You can tell me anything, I hope you know that. And listen, it's okay to be sad. You have a lot of emotions right now." She tucks a loose strand of hair behind her ear, her gaze never leaving Nico's face. "And although I don't know the full story, I do know that everyone struggles. Nico, look at me. Everyone struggles."

She lets out a little sigh, as if she's about to share a secret just between them. "Who knows, your friends might be having big feelings right now too." Her hands rest gently in her lap, a silent reminder that she's here, solid and real. "We really never know what other people are going through," she adds, her voice a soft murmur that fills the room with quiet understanding.

Nico watches his stand up, ready to tackle her own day, yet making it clear she's never too far away. His mind whirls with thoughts, but for now, he clings to the lifeline she's thrown him. Maybe, just maybe, he isn't alone in this boat of tangled emotions after all.

Nico tugs the corner of his comforter, making a tent over his head. "You are right, Mom," he mumbles into the soft folds of his blanket fortress. The words feel heavy, which make him sink deeper into the pillows piled up around him.

As she closes the door behind her, Nico allows himself a small exhale. He tries to imagine what he'd be doing right now if things were different—if his friends hadn't turned against him, if the controller was still in his hands. Adventures would unfold at the press of a button, worlds would open up, ready to explore. But those thoughts don't help. They just add more weight to an already too-heavy heart.

The afternoon drags on, each minute stretching longer than the last. Nico flips onto his side, hugging his favorite pillow.

With a sigh, he closes his eyes, letting the sounds of the house wrap around him—the distant tap-tap of his mom's keyboard downstairs, the creak of the stairs when she takes a break to stretch her legs, the comforting rhythm of home.

Late in the afternoon, the door to Nico's room creaks open, and a sliver of the outside world sneaks in alongside his sister. Piper's presence is like a burst of sunlight through gloomy clouds as she bounds toward his bed with the energy of a happy puppy who just wants to play.

"Guess what I've got!" she exclaims, her voice bubbling with excitement. In her hand, she clutches something that instantly makes Nico's heart do a hopeful little somersault—a sugar cookie, its edges perfectly golden, as if baked with him in mind.

"They had them in the cafeteria today," Piper says, presenting the treat like a trophy. "I know how much you like them, so I saved it for you."

For a moment, Nico forgets about his troubles. The mere sight of the cookie, dotted with colorful sprinkles, sends a wave of contentment through him. It's not just a cookie—it's a gesture of sisterly love, a sprinkle-covered sign that he's not alone.

"Thanks, Piper," he says, his voice thick with gratitude. Something swells inside him, a mix of affection and appreciation for this pint-sized ally who understands the importance of sugar-frosted yumminess.

He reaches out, pulling her into a hug that's as sweet as the treat she's brought him. Piper wraps her arms around him, and for a brief moment, all is right in his world.

"I'm glad you're feeling better," she whispers with a wink, as if they're co-conspirators in chasing away the blues.

Nico nods, a smile breaking through like the first rays of dawn after a stormy night. He knows there are still challenges ahead, but with Piper by his side, maybe they won't seem quite so big.

Nico brushes the last crumbs of the sugar cookie from his fingers. The afternoon sun casts long shadows in his room, hinting at the golden hour just before dinner, the perfect time for one of their favorite activities.

"Hey, how about another game of ping-pong tennis in the backyard?" Nico asks, already picturing the setup. Their creative game is a wild mash-up of rules, part ping-pong, part tennis, and entirely their invention.

Piper's eyes light up, her enthusiasm infectious. "I thought you'd never ask!" she replies with a grin that matches Nico's own.

They scramble to their feet, racing each other to the back door. Piper's laughter rings out, a melody that makes the weight on Nico's shoulders feel a little lighter. He can't help but laugh too, the feeling bubbling up from somewhere deep inside.

In the backyard, the net is a bit crooked, and the paddles have seen better days, but none of that matters. They volley back and forth, the ping-pong ball zipping through the air, creating its own rhythm as it bounces from paddle to grass and back again. Each hit is a small victory, a pushback against the day's earlier troubles.

"Take that!" Nico teases as he sends a tricky spin shot Piper's way.

"Nice try!" she counters, dancing to the side to return it with her own flair.

The game goes on, the score forgotten as they play for the sheer thrill of it. With each swing, each step, and each shared giggle, Nico feels a bit more like himself. It's not just a game—it's a reminder that friendship, even if it's with your quirky younger sister, is a kind of magic all on its own.

CHAPTER 11
Friends First

Nico's sneakers squeak against the freshly waxed floors of Sunnyville Elementary as he makes his way through the crowded halls. A bundle of nerves and hurt balled up inside him like a crumpled piece of homework. He spots Emma and Lucas by their lockers, laughing about something in Lucas's notebook. Nico's heart sinks a little further. They haven't even noticed he's gone.

"Hey," he says, a bit louder than intended. The laughter stops. Emma and Lucas look up, surprise etched on their faces.

"What's up, Nico?" Emma asks, her voice laced with concern as she takes in his troubled expression.

"Can we talk? Just for a minute." His gaze flickers between the two, settling on the controller peeking from Lucas's backpack—a reminder of the rift it caused.

"Sure, man," Lucas says, leaning against the lockers with a casual ease that Nico envies.

"Look, I miss hanging out with you both," Nico starts, his voice shaky but gaining strength. "And...and I just want to say that our friendship means more to me than any stupid game controller."

Emma's smile is soft, and her eyes are kind—like always. "We miss you too, Nico," she says, reaching out to squeeze his arm reassuringly.

Lucas nods, but there's a flicker of something else in his expression. "That's true. The game isn't everything," he admits, though it sounds like he's trying to convince himself just as much as Nico.

"Right," Nico agrees, feeling a sense of relief. "Friends first, okay?"

"Friends first," they echo, and Nico manages to muster a half-smile. It's not all fixed, not yet, but it's a start. A new level in their real-life adventure, ready to be played together.

Nico fidgets with the hem of his shirt like he usually does when he is feeling uneasy. He watches as Emma's face crumples with guilt. Lucas shifts from one foot to another, his eyes darting away before locking back onto Nico's.

"Sorry," Emma blurts out, her voice laced with regret. "We didn't mean to make you feel left out. It's just... that controller seemed to change you. It was as if you were suddenly so much cooler than us."

Lucas clears his throat, stepping forward. "Yeah, we got carried away with our own feelings of envy," he confesses, running a hand through his spiky hair. "Shouldn't have let it get between us."

"Me too," Nico says, his words tumbling out in a rush. "I was so hyped about the superpower stuff; I forgot what really mattered." He takes a deep breath, feeling lighter. "I'm putting down the controller. For real this time."

Emma's smile returns, warmer now, and even Lucas looks relieved. They all exchange nods, an unspoken agreement sealing their mended friendship.

Later that afternoon, Nico flops onto the grass in his backyard, Piper plopping down beside him. She plucks at the blades of grass, twirling them between her fingers.

"Hey, you okay?" she asks, her green eyes reflecting concern mixed with curiosity.

Nico nods, then shrugs. "Yeah, just thinking about today."

"Real-life adventures are way cooler than any game," Piper says with a grin, a smudge of dirt on her cheek like a badge of honor. "You should've seen the frog I found!" He turns to look at his sister, noticing the way her eyes light up when she talks about her day exploring the creek behind their house.

Nico chuckles, imagining Piper's excitement over her discovery. Her enthusiasm is endearing, filling him with a sense of wonder for the world outside screens and pixels.

"Look at us," Piper gestures around their backyard—the trees rustling in the wind, birds chirping melodies, and the sun playing hide and seek behind fluffy clouds. "This is our open-world game. We can go on real quests, find hidden treasures, and you don't need any magic controller for that."

Nico sits up, intrigued by the idea. He imagines himself as the hero of his own story—no fancy gadgets, just his wits and Piper by his side. It sounds epic.

"I like making my own adventures, but sometimes real life is too hard" he admits.

"That's so true!" Piper exclaims. "But you're strong. You've got your brains, a hunger for curiosity, and I think you're pretty fun to be around. And with my rockstar personality—we're unstoppable!"

They both laugh, the sound mingling with the breeze. The idea is thrilling, like unlocking a new level in a game, but better because it's real.

"Promise we'll make up another new game tomorrow?" Nico says, suddenly eager to embark on this new adventure.

"Promise," Piper agrees, pinky-swearing for extra certainty.

"Good. We could use some fresh air." Nico grins. "We definitely need to touch grass more often."

"Totally!" Piper giggles, and they both fall back onto the grass, looking up at the sky, plotting future escapades.

Their laughter floats up, joining the symphony of the great outdoors—a reminder that the best levels are still waiting to be explored, controller-free.

Nico marches up to his room, determination leading the way. He's on a mission, one that doesn't require any digital dexterity or intense maneuvers on the screen. The magical controller, once a token of unlimited possibilities, feels heavy in his hand—a weight he's ready to set aside.

"Goodbye, crazy adventures," he mutters to himself, sifting through his closet for the perfect hiding spot. Stacks of comic books and action figures watch silently as Nico takes out the lockbox he found in the garage days earlier. It's the final resting place for the device that brought him so much joy— and just as much trouble.

He wipes off the top of the box and gently places the controller inside. The wooden flaps fold over with a soft thud, sealing away the magic. "I'm done with all that magic!" Nico declares to the quiet of his room, the pile of laundry on the floor a testament to his resolve.

Piper pokes her head around the door. "But how will you play video games?" she asks, her voice tinged with concern for her brother's sudden change of heart.

Nico spins around, a spark of excitement replacing the solemn moment. "I'll take a break for now." He strides over to his desk, where his neglected laptop sits closed next to a microphone stand. "Besides, my YouTube channel could use some love."

"Really?" Piper steps into the room, her presence like a burst of sunshine through the open window.

"Yep." Nico nods, opening the laptop and waking it from its slumber. The screen lights up, revealing a background of his YouTube logo. "Want to help me plan my videos?" he asks, turning towards Piper with an expectant smile.

"Of course!" Piper exclaims, bouncing on the balls of her feet. She's always admired Nico's passion for creating content, and being part of it feels like joining an exclusive club—the kind of club that crafts epic tales and shares them with the world.

"Awesome." Nico grins, scooting over to make room for Piper at the desk. Together, they're about to embark on a new journey—

one filled with creativity, camaraderie, and maybe even a few bloopers along the way.

Piper clutches her hands, a secret wish blooming inside her. "That controller is proving to be more magical than I ever could have imagined," she whispers, so low it's almost lost in the hum of the computer.

She spins on her heel, her curly hair dancing around her shoulders as she faces Nico with determination shining in her bright green eyes. "I cannot wait to help!" Her voice is filled with enthusiasm, as if she's just been handed the lead role in the school play. She dashes out of the room, her feet barely touching the ground.

"Wait here!" she calls over her shoulder, her words trailing behind like a kite tail caught on a breeze.

She returns in a flash, clutching a notebook. It's covered in stickers—unicorns, rainbows, and shimmering stars—each one placed with care to create a collage of her vibrant personality. She flips it open to reveal pages adorned with doodles, each one a testament to her boundless creativity.

"Let's brainstorm some epic video ideas," Piper says, plopping down next to Nico, excitement bubbling through her like a fizzy soda.

Nico can't help but grin at his sister's perpetual energy. With Piper's artistic flair and his knack for gaming, they're about to create something truly special. Together, they are an unstoppable team, ready to conquer the digital world—one impressive video at a time.

CHAPTER 12
Sunshine Before Screen time

The camera wobbles for a moment before Nico steadies it, a wide grin spreading across his face. "Ready, Piper?" he calls out.

"Born ready!" Piper chirps from off-screen, her voice bubbling with excitement. She bursts into frame, curls bouncing, green eyes alight with the thrill of performance. With a flair for the dramatic, she launches into a perfectly timed backflip that would make any gymnast proud.

"Whoa!" Nico exclaims, and the viewers can almost see his blue eyes widening behind the lens. He zooms in just as Piper sticks the landing, her arms thrown high in triumph. The siblings share a look, an unspoken agreement that this is what fun looks like.

"Your turn, Nico!" Piper urges, her voice a playful challenge.

Nico sets the camera on the trusty tripod, ensuring their audience has a front-row seat to the Carmichael siblings' living room turned adventure land. He takes a deep breath, channels his inner acrobat, and with a running start, executes an aerial that's more enthusiastic than graceful. But it's the effort that counts, and their laughter fills the room, contagious and genuine.

"What's going on in there" Mr. Carmichael's voice can be heard calling from the other room.

"Nothing!" the two children say in unison then giggle quietly.

"Okay, okay," Nico pants, ruffling his messy blonde hair as he regains his balance, "Let's dial up the wow factor." He rummages through a box of props and gadgets, the detritus of countless video adventures. He pulls out a deck of cards and waggles his eyebrows at Piper. "Prepare to be amazed!"

"Bring on the magic, Nico!" Piper cheers, clapping her hands in anticipation.

With a quick shuffle and a flick of his wrist, Nico makes cards appear and disappear with the finesse of a pint-sized Houdini. Piper's eyes follow every movement, occasionally glancing at the camera to ensure their online friends are getting the best view.

"Time for the grand finale!" Nico proclaims, setting the cards aside. He reaches for their homemade volcano experiment, a concoction of baking soda and vinegar waiting for its explosive moment of fame. "Science meets spectacle!"

Piper nods, her role as the eager assistant never wavering. Together, they count down, "Three, two, one!" and Nico pours the vinegar into the crater. A fountain of frothy lava erupts, spilling over the papier-mâché mountain and onto the table with a satisfying fizz.

"Wowzers!" Piper exclaims, clapping her hands with glee.

"Did you see that?!" Nico asks the camera, his voice thick with wonder and pride. He knows the comments section will blow up with emojis and exclamations.

As the final bubbles pop and the laughter subsides, Piper and Nico give each other a high-five, their bond as siblings and co-conspirators in fun stronger than ever. Their videos are more than just play; they're memories in the making, digital records of joy and discovery, liked and shared by friends unseen but always there.

"Thanks for watching," they chorus, waving at the camera before Nico reaches out to end the recording. The screen goes black, but their adventure is far from over.

That weekend, the rain drums a steady beat on the windowpane, the gray clouds streaking the glass and blurring the world outside. Inside, Nico Carmichael eyes the droplets with a distant look, the kind that speaks of longing for sunnier days and outdoor adventures. His short, messy blonde hair is tousled more than usual today, as if in silent protest against the gloomy weather.

"Hey, Piper," he calls out, his voice tinged with a hint of restlessness. "Do you ever miss just... chilling and playing games?" He spins a basketball on his fingertip—a trick they practiced last week for a video—then catches it with a sigh.

Piper, sprawled across the living room rug with a comic book, glances up. She studies her brother and nods slowly. "Sometimes," she admits, remembering the hours they'd lose to quests and online battles, controllers gripped tightly in their hands.

Nico sets the basketball aside, the thud muted by the carpet.

"Mom!" he calls instead, pivoting towards the kitchen. "Can I get a new video game controller?"

From the other room, the clatter of dishes pauses, and Mrs. Carmichael's voice floats back to him, curious and a touch amused. "What's wrong with your other one?" There's an unassuming tone in her question, a gentle prod that suggests she is completely unaware of the magic controller's tricks and quirks.

Nico bites his lip, wrestling with his desire for the familiar comfort of a normal controller in his hands, untainted by the antics of their online shenanigans. He loves the fun and creativity they pour into their channel, but today, the rainy-day blues have him yearning for simpler times when he could just game without any surprises.

"Uh, it's acting weird," Nico replies, hopefulness weaving through his words like the perfect cheat code for unlocking his mom's heart.

Nico taps his foot against the hardwood floor, the rhythm echoing his restless thoughts. He glances at the controller again, its buttons and joysticks too quiet on this dreary afternoon. Mrs. Carmichael leans against the doorframe, arms crossed, her gentle eyes studying him with a mix of patience and curiosity.

"Mom," Nico starts, shifting his weight from one foot to the other, "I've had that controller for almost a year." It feels as if the controller is miles away, instead of safely tucked away in the same room. "Anyway, it's uh, not working correctly."

Mrs. Carmichael raises an eyebrow, her lips curving into a knowing smile. She knows all about the mischief that controller has caused, the unexpected turns in their gaming adventures that were fun at first but now leave Nico craving the ordinary.

"Is that so?" she says, stepping closer. The scent of fresh cookies, still warm from the oven, wafts from behind her. "Seems like it was working just fine a week or so ago."

"Yeah, kind of…" Cheeks flushing, his voice trails off, hoping his mom will cave like she is almost always known to do.

"Alright," she finally says, turning back to face him with a decision in her eyes. "You can get a new controller."

Nico's face lights up, wondering how it could have been that easy. But as he's about to leap for joy, she holds up a hand.

"But," she continues, a serious note threading through her voice, "you're going to pay for it by earning the money."

His excitement deflates a little. But then he straightens up, determination setting into his features. If there's one thing he's good at, it's facing challenges head-on. "Okay. Thanks, Mom," he says, nodding more to himself than to her. "I'll figure something out."

Mrs. Carmichael smiles warmly at him, proud of her son's resolve. "I know you will," she says, and with another look at him, she adds, "Sometimes the best adventures are the ones we work the hardest for."

Nico slumps onto his beanbag chair with a sigh, feeling the burden of his new mission. His magic controller had seen more action than a knight's armor—each mark and flaw a reminder of virtual and real-life adventure, a testament to challenges and victories. But now it's useless as a doorstop.

"Hey, don't look so glum," Piper chirps as she twirls into his room. She plants herself cross-legged on the carpet, her green eyes sparkling with the kind of optimism that can only come from someone who still believes in fairy tale endings. "We'll get you that new controller. Team Carmichael never backs down from a challenge, right?"

Nico can't help but crack a smile. "Right," he echoes, though his mind is racing like a hamster in a wheel. How does an eleven-year-old make a hundred dollars? He imagines himself trying to sell lemonade in the rain or washing cars during a thunderstorm—not the most practical plans.

"Okay, idea time." Piper claps her hands together, her excitement infectious. "You're super good at gaming and I can sing and dance. We could put on a show! Or maybe a big garage sale?"

"In the rain?" Nico asks, rolling his eyes, already picturing the disaster that would be.

"How about a bake sale!" Piper says, already loving the idea of spending the day baking her favorite goodies.

Nico shook his head suggesting a firm no. Last time they tried to make cookies, they ended up with something closer to charcoal briquettes than chocolate chip.

"Umm, let's stick to what we're good at," Nico says, saving them both from a repeat performance. "Maybe we can do more videos? Like tutorials or challenges?" Nico says, warming up to the brainstorming session.

"Challenges are good!" Piper bounces slightly, excited by the idea. "People love those. Especially if there's something wacky or weird involved!"

"Like eating a spoonful of hot sauce while reciting the alphabet backwards?" Nico offers with a mischievous glint behind his glasses.

"Exactly!" Piper laughs, high-fiving her brother. "And every view gets us closer to your new controller."

"Yes!" Nico says, a new sense of purpose filling him. Together, they start plotting out ideas, their minds buzzing with notions that are just crazy enough to work.

"Let's do this," Piper declares, feeling that familiar thrill of adventure, energizing Nico with the hope of possibilities.

CHAPTER 13
Making Money

The next evening, there's a bounce in Nico's step, a leftover habit from all the gymnastics training, but even that feels off today. With each step, he replays the day's practice in his mind—the stumbles, the slips, the missed cues. The competition is looming, and his routine feels more like a tangle of limbs than an elegant display of skill.

"Come on, Nico," he whispers to himself, trying to muster some of that go-get-'em attitude that usually fuels him. He stops in front of the mirror, hands on his hips, expression slightly askew. "You've got this."

But the reflection staring back doesn't seem convinced. He straightens his shoulders and attempts a determined nod, but it's half-hearted.

"Who am I kidding?" He groans, plopping down at his desk. The thought of his magic controller just steps away in the back of his closet seems to smirk at him, and he can't help but feel like it's another reminder of things falling apart.

"Okay, plan B," he says, hopeful despite the odds. "Extra chores? Babysitting Alfie? Dog walking? Shoveling snow" Each option flits through his mind, but they all require something he's short on—time. Plus, snow wasn't in the forecast for a few more weeks.

With gymnastics eating up most of his evenings, there's hardly a moment to spare for moneymaking schemes. And now, with his confidence in doing a perfect aerial at an all-time low, Nico wonders if he'll ever find his footing again, let alone earn enough cash for a new controller.

"Something's gotta give," he murmurs, more to the universe than to himself. Nico can't shake the feeling that he's stuck, caught between the need to level up in the virtual world and the pressure to stick the landing in the real one.

Nico slumps in front of his computer, the glow from the screen flickering across his furrowed brow. He clicks refresh on his YouTube channel, hoping for a spike in views that just isn't there. His latest video—a combo of his best gaming moments and some awesome gymnastics flips—sits at a measly thirty-two views after two days.

"Come on," he mutters under his breath, as if coaxing the numbers to climb right before his eyes. But they remain stubbornly low, a digital thumbs-down to his efforts. He scans the comments, hoping for some sort of encouragement but finds only a desert of interaction. No likes, no "Great job, Nico!" not even a random "First!" from an eager fan. Just empty space beneath his hard work.

He leans back in his chair, pushing his homework aside with a sigh. The excitement that used to bubble up within him every time he powered on his console or leaped onto the gymnastics mat has fizzed out like a forgotten soda. Now, each flip feels heavier, each game less thrilling, without the familiar hum of his favorite controller in his hands.

"Maybe I'm losing my touch," he whispers, half to the room, half to the part of himself that's scared it might be true. The videos were supposed to be fun, an extra sprinkle of awesome on top of everything else he loves. But now, as the view counter stagnates, doubt creeps in, whispering that maybe the world isn't as eager to watch him succeed as he thought.

"Or maybe they just don't care anymore," he adds, the words tasting bitter. He pushes away from the desk, the chair rolling back with a creak that seems to echo his frustration. Nico paces his room, each step a heavy drumbeat marking the rhythm of his faltering confidence.

"Maybe I'm just not good enough," he admits to the emptiness around him. He thinks of his controller, gathering dust in the closet. Once a portal to endless possibilities, now just a reminder of what seems impossible to reach. Can he ever bring back the magic, or has the game changed without him?

Nico shakes his head, trying to dislodge the negative thoughts. He needs a plan, a new strategy to reclaim the excitement and connect once again with the joy he knows is still there, somewhere. But how?

"Can't let this stop me," Nico tells himself, though the fight in his voice is waning. He grabs a pair of socks from the floor and tosses them into the hamper—a small victory in the midst of his growing anxieties.

In the silence of his room, surrounded by his favorite things and shelves lined with trophies that seem to mock him now, Nico feels the weight of expectation bearing down. It's a pressure cooker of "what ifs" and "not good enoughs" simmering beneath the surface.

"Got to get back in the game," he decides, even if he's not quite sure how. He knows one thing for certain: he can't win back the excitement or the viewers or nail that gymnastics routine without believing in himself first. And that's one high score that seems harder and harder to beat.

Nico's room is dim, the only light a soft glow from the streetlamp outside filtering through his curtains. He sits on the edge of his bed, the silence around him almost too loud. His once comforting space now feels like a cavern, each of his collectibles and action figures staring back at him with a challenge he's not sure he can meet.

He stands up, pushing the chair back with a squeak, and heads over to his closet. Maybe there's something in there he can sell, some forgotten treasure that'll be worth its weight in dollars. He starts rummaging through old toys and dusty board games, looking for a glimmer of hope among the cobwebs.

"Come on, Nico," he mutters to himself, trying to summon that spark of determination Miss Jenkin always talks about in class. But tonight, it's as elusive as the viewers on his YouTube channel. He eyes the lockbox, the home of his magical controller, that magical piece of technology that once held so much promise, calling to him from its spot hidden away. "Maybe just a quick look," he thinks.

"Okay," he whispers to himself, a soft declaration in the solitude of his room. With a deep breath, trying to shake off the heaviness of his thoughts, he reaches for the lockbox and opens it carefully.

Inside, the controller sits. When he sees it, a wave of emotions come over him. He feels anxious, excited, hopeful and a sense of guilt. The controller looks so mundane there, just another piece of plastic, but Nico knows better. He pauses, letting the memories flood back—the victories, the laughter, the rush of being unbeatable and even popular. Those were the days.

With a tentative hand, he picks up the box and cradles it in his arms. The cardboard feels rough against his skin, a stark contrast to the smooth surface he remembers.

Gently, like uncovering a treasure, he lifts the lid and there it lies: the controller.

It seems to recognize him, responding to his touch. The moment his fingers brush against it, the gadget lights up, glowing with the promise of a world he can control. The buttons shine under the warm light of his room, eager for action.

"Wow..." Nico can't help but smile, the sight sparking a flicker of hope in his heart. The controller still has its magic, it seems, ready to transport him to worlds where he can be the hero once again. Maybe, just maybe, he can find his way back to the excitement he's been missing.

Carefully, he lifts it from the box, feeling the familiar weight in his hands. The glow from the controller casts dancing shadows around the room. In this moment, with the controller pulsing with life, anything feels possible.

"Come on," he tells it quietly, a grin spreading across his face. "Let's see what we can do."

Nico's heart races with a mix of nerves and excitement as he grips the controller, its buttons so comfortable in his grasp. The thought of what could happen next sends a shiver down his spine; it's as if he's on the edge of a digital cliff, about to leap into the unknown.

"Okay," he whispers to himself, summoning courage. He reaches for his wallet, pulling out a crumpled dollar bill that smells faintly of bubble gum and school cafeteria lunches.

Holding his breath, Nico positions the controller over the bill, his thumb hovering over the button that feels like it's pulsing under his skin. The light from the controller casts a strange, otherworldly glow on the greenback, making the familiar face of

George Washington look like he's about to embark on an adventure of his own.

"Here goes nothing," he mutters, more to the controller than to himself, and clicks the button.

In a flash of light so bright it makes him squint, the dollar bill quivers as if alive. When the light fades, the bill lies transformed before him—a crisp, new $100 bill staring up at him in all its glory, its ink sharp against the paper.

"Whoa!" Nico's voice cracks in amazement, "That's what I'm talking about!"

A giant grin splits his face, the kind that hasn't appeared for weeks. For a moment, the worries about boredom, gymnastics competitions, and YouTube views evaporate, replaced by a rush of exhilaration that courses through his veins.

"Is this real life?" he asks the room, half expecting his trophies to answer back. He picks up the bill, turning it over in his hands, examining each intricate detail with wide, disbelieving eyes behind his glasses.

"Or is this just fantasy?" he sings under his breath, chuckling at his own reference, feeling for once that he's got the upper hand in a game that's been stacking the odds against him.

Nico's room buzzes with the energy of a newfound secret, a sense of triumph radiating from him as he clutches the transformed bill. He's still reeling from the magic when the door bursts open without warning.

Piper bounds in, her bright green eyes wide with excitement and oblivious to the scene she's interrupting. "Who are you talking to?" she asks, head tilting like one of those curious puppies from the cartoons they used to watch together on Saturday mornings.

"Can't you knock?" Nico snaps, his voice sharper than he intends. The annoyance ripples through him, disturbing the afterglow of his victory. Piper recoils slightly, her initial enthusiasm dimming like a stage light flickering out.

"Sorry..." She stumbles over the word, looking like she might bolt at any second. But she plants her feet, determined. "I had an idea I wanted to share with you," she says, regaining a bit of her earlier spark, though it's clear she's shaken by his outburst.

Nico can't help but feel a twinge of guilt seeing her startled expression. After all, Piper has been by his side a lot lately. And, her ideas have often turned their most mundane afternoons into adventures brimming with laughter and spontaneous dance-offs. But right now, he's not in the mood for brainstorming or sisterly bonding; he's got a ticket to freedom in his hand, and that's all that matters.

Piper's eyes dart to the corner of Nico's desk, where the glow of the controller catches her attention like a beacon. "Why are you so angry—oh my gosh!" Her voice rises in pitch as realization dawns on her small, expressive face. She takes a hesitant step forward, her wonder growing with each move. "Are you using the controller?" Disappointment tinges her words, painting them a shade sadder than her usual sunny demeanor.

He snatches the controller, cradling it against his chest protectively before shoving it out of sight behind him. "No," he lies, his words coming out more forceful than he intends. The controller's secret—their secret—is out now, and he feels the weight of betrayal heavy on his shoulders.

"Get out!" he screams, louder than necessary, louder than he ever yells at Piper. His hands tremble behind him, not just from the lie but from the fear of losing this newfound power, this escape he's desperately clinging to.

Piper's lips quiver, tears welling up in her bright green eyes that usually shine with creativity and mischief. But now, they're just pools of hurt, reflecting back the harshness of his shout. Without another word, she turns on her heel, her small frame shaking with silent sobs as she flees the room.

The door slams shut behind her, leaving Nico alone with the pulsing light of the controller and the hollow echo of his sister's crying. A twinge of regret stabs at him, sharper than the edge of any video game sword. He didn't mean to make her cry; he never does. But with every new level of excitement the controller brings, it seems he's pushing away the very people he loves most.

CHAPTER 14
New Controller in Town

Today is Saturday, the best day of the week. It's free from school responsibilities and full of possibilities! And today, it's even better because Nico has exactly one hundred reasons to be happy—all adding up to the freshly printed $100 bill in his piggy bank.

Rolling out of bed, he's on a mission. Today he gets a brand-new video game controller for gaming only, no magic. The thought alone fuels his energetic leap into his jeans and t-shirt, still grass stained from his adventures with Piper.

"Morning, Mom!" Nico chirps as he bounds into the kitchen, where Mrs. Carmichael stands by the counter, sipping her coffee. Her gentle eyes lift from her mug, a warm smile spreading across her face at the sight of his enthusiasm.

"Good morning, sweetie! You're in a good mood today," she remarks, tucking a strand of shoulder-length hair behind her ear.

"Yep! I've got big plans!" Nico says, patting his pocket. He wonders, with a twinge of excitement, if this new controller might carry a touch of magic just like the old one. As he hands the money to his mom, her eyebrows raise in surprise.

"Where'd you get that?" Mr. Carmichael asks, examining the large bill.

Nico grins, a mischievous glint in his eye. "I guess you could say, it just magically appeared," he tells her.

Mrs. Carmichael chuckles, shaking her head at her son's creative explanation. She knew how well her son was at saving his birthday money and monetary gifts from relatives. "Well then, we'll see what kind of 'magic' we can find at the store later. But, why don't you use your gift card?"

"Gift card?" Nico questions.

"Remember? The one you were planning to use for a new gaming console but didn't have to use because Aunt Louise got it for you. I think there's at least $100 on that," Mrs. Carmichael says, suggesting an alternative.

"Oh, yeah! Awesome!" Nico says, feeling very relieved that he could buy a new controller in an honest way. He pumps his fist in the air, already imagining the epic gaming sessions to come. With a new controller in his hands, he'd be unstoppable. And who knows? Maybe it really would be magical.

The air hums with the quiet promise of adventure, and sunlight dances through the open window, casting a warm glow over the half-eaten bowl of cereal in front of him. Mrs. Carmichael leans against the counter, her eyes softening as she watches her son with a blend of amusement and pride. Then, she collects the $100 bill.

"Nico, you've always been such a careful saver," she says, tucking the bill into her purse without another moment's hesitation. "But a bill of this size, should probably stay in a safer spot other than your room."

"I promise I'll keep it safe," Nico assures her.

"It's no problem. I'm going to the bank later, I'll put it in your savings account for you to take out later," Mrs. Carmichael says, despite his plea.

The enchanted $100 bill made Nico uneasy, so he doesn't protest. All he can think of now are the aisles of the electronic store, each shelf lined with gadgets and gizmos sparkling under the fluorescent lights. His new controller is waiting there—just out of reach for now, but soon to be his. The very thought has him bouncing on the balls of his feet, eager to set off on this mini quest.

"Thanks, Mom!" he exclaims, already picturing himself unwrapping the shiny packaging of his much-anticipated purchase. Then he adds, "Can I invite Lucas to come shopping with us?"

"Of course," Mrs. Carmichael says, happy that her son and his best friend have made amends.

"Check this one out!" Lucas points to a display with a controller encased in glass, its surface a dance of colors changing with every angle. It's the kind of controller that doesn't just respond to your touch; it seems to know your next move before you make it.

"Wow, Nico! You're going to win all the games with this one!" Lucas says, his voice echoing with genuine awe.

"Only if my skills can keep up," Nico replies, then continues to walk down the aisle.

"Hey, aren't you going to get it?" Lucas wonders.

"Nah, I'm going to buy the same one I've always had," Nico says, unbothered by the rows of flashy controllers.

"Dude, you've got like $200 on that gift card. Why not splurge a little?" Lucas encourages, hoping for the opportunity to come over and play.

Nico rejects the idea and picks the same controller as before. They both take the chosen controller off its stand, holding the possibility of winning in their hands.

"Let's go conquer some leaderboards," Nico declares, a surge of adrenaline pumping through him at the thought of the battles ahead and the stories they'll tell.

Lucas agrees, feeling the excitement, his clever mind already planning strategies and moves. They go to the cashier, their laughter blending with the electronic sounds that fill the air. Nico thinks that today is the beginning of something special—a new adventure, a new device in his gaming collection, and a new memory made with his friend beside him.

Nico's hand smacks into Lucas's with a satisfying clap that resonates through the bustling store. "As long as you're on my team!" he exclaims, his grin spreading from ear to ear. The new controller feels comfortable in his grip, like it's been waiting for him all along.

"Deal!" Lucas replies, returning the high five with equal enthusiasm. Together, they make an unbeatable duo, and Nico can hardly wait to test out their teamwork with the shiny new addition to his gaming gear.

Nico rushes to the door of his house, holding the new controller under his arm. He opens the door, feeling welcomed by the familiar and comforting scent of home. He's eager to share his day with Piper and show her his purchase. Maybe she'll even be interested in seeing him play later.

He skips up the stairs two at a time, bursting with excitement, but then he stops short. Through the half-open door across the hall, he sees Piper in her room, her body curled up on the bed. Her shoulders tremble, and Nico's heart does a somersault.

It's not often that he catches sight of his sister looking anything less than happy.

"Hey, Pip! What's up?" he calls out, his voice still laced with the happiness of his own day, but it falters when he sees the glisten of tears on her cheeks. He takes a tentative step toward her, the joy of his new purchase dimming in the light of his sister's distress.

Piper's voice quivers, each word piercing through the carefree bubble Nico's been floating in all day. "You have been so mean to me lately. You were so mean last night!" she chokes out, her small hands quickly swiping at the damp trails on her cheeks. The room feels suddenly still, the air heavy with her accusation. "And it's all because of those stupid video games!"

The words hang there, suspended like a jump in one of Nico's platformers where the hero freezes mid-air before the inevitable fall. For a moment, he's speechless, his mouth opening and closing without sound. He can't remember the last time he actually looked at Piper—not just saw her in passing, but really looked at her.

A warm flush of guilt creeps up Nico's neck, coloring his pale cheeks a bright pink. It's a strange feeling, prickling under his skin, making him squirm. But then, just as quickly, the warmth retreats, leaving behind a chilly void. His stomach plummets, the excitement from earlier evaporating.

It's as if he's swallowed one of those spiky seed balls that litter their backyard in the fall—sharp and uncomfortable. They always stick to your socks when you're not looking, a nuisance that's hard to shake off. And right now, Nico feels that same irritating poke in the pit of his belly, a reminder of something he can't ignore any longer.

Nico inches closer to his sister, the spiky sensation in his stomach now a dull throb.

He crouches beside her bed, his gaze softening as he looks at her tear-streaked face. "I'm so sorry, Piper," he murmurs, his voice barely above a whisper.

Piper hesitates for a moment, her bright green eyes searching Nico's blue ones for sincerity. Then, slowly, she turns her head towards him, the hint of a sniffle still lingering in the air. With a small nod, she accepts his apology.

"Really, I am," Nico adds, reaching out to envelop her in a gentle hug. His arms wrap around her small frame, and he can feel her body relax as she leans into his embrace. Piper, with her big heart and boundless forgiveness, doesn't hold grudges for long.

After a minute, he pulls back, ruffling her curly hair playfully. Standing up, he can't help but feel lighter, like that nasty feeling of guilt has been lifted and carried away. "Now, let's go play some video games!"

Nico announces with renewed cheer, already bounding across the hallway to his room.

Piper trails behind him, wiping the last remnants of tears from her cheeks, a tentative smile tugging at her lips. As they enter Nico's gaming sanctuary, Piper pauses, her voice tinged with concern.

"Now that you have the new controller, promise me you won't use the other one, okay?" Her request hangs between them, an earnest plea wrapped in hope.

Nico nods, the weight of his promise settling firmly on his shoulders. "Okay," he agrees, eager to make things right. The magic controller, once an object of wonder, now feels like a relic of past missteps; it's time to turn the page on that chapter.

Together, they flop onto the beanbag chairs, the screen lighting up with vibrant colors as

Nico powers on the console. Side by side, the siblings are ready to embark on digital adventures, their bond stronger than any game level they could conquer.

Nico's fingers hover over the shiny buttons of the new controller, a grin plastered on his face. It feels right in his hands—sturdy, responsive, and full of promise for epic gameplays ahead. But as he glances at Piper, her green eyes wide and earnest, he can sense her worry.

"Sure, Pip," Nico says, his tone softening. He unplugs the controller with its mystical allure and opens the top drawer of his desk, sliding it into a corner where it won't tempt him—or cause any more trouble. "It's put away. I don't think I'll need it for a while anyway." His words feel like a silent vow to focus on what truly matters: real-life adventures with his sister.

Satisfied, Piper claps her hands together, the sound echoing lightly. The two siblings share a look, an unspoken understanding passing between them. Today is about fresh starts and having fun the old-fashioned way—with each other's company.

CHAPTER 15
Balancing Act

Nico hovers on the edge of his chair, the glow from his screen casting a warm light across his eager face. He's just completed another level, a digital victory that usually keeps his fingers glued to the buttons. But today, something stirs inside him, a yearning for something beyond the screen.

"Life is an adventure," he tells himself, saying the words over and over. He shuts off the game with a firm click.

He throws on his favorite hoodie and runs outside to do some flips on the family trampoline. Alfie trails behind him.

"Whoa, I'm still good at this!" he exclaims, surprised by his own ease. Nico has always loved how gymnastics makes him feel like he's flying, defying gravity with each leap and tumble. The joy bubbling up inside him is different from winning a game; it's real and it's all his.

After a few more flips, he pauses, panting lightly. He smiles, knowing he can make many more friends in this endless world. At school the next day, he joins a new group of kids at the playground. They're gathered around a collection of marbles, brightly colored orbs that catch the sunlight in their glassy surfaces.

"Can I try?" Nico asks, curiosity piqued by this simple yet captivating pastime.

"Sure, Nico! Here, have some of mine to start with," a friendly classmate offers, sliding a handful of marbles toward him.

The marbles feel cool and smooth in his palm, a tangible thrill. He flicks his first marble into the circle, watching it knock against the others with a satisfying clink. Laughter bubbles up around him as they cheer on each other's attempts, the camaraderie infectious.

"Hey, you're pretty good at this," one of the kids notes, impressed by Nico's beginner's luck.

"Thanks," Nico replies, grinning wider than he has in weeks. "It's fun trying new things."

As children line up, signaling the end of recess, Nico feels a sense of contentment. New friendships are forming, new hobbies are taking root, and his love for gaming now shares space with the vibrant world around him.

"Life's got its own levels to beat," he thinks to himself, tucking the marbles into his pocket, a treasure trove of new memories. "And I'm just getting started."

Nico vaults over the park bench, landing with a bounce. Lucas and Emma are already there, waiting for him with their bikes propped against the old oak tree that's seen countless summers come and go. It's a challenge they concocted together: a race through the winding paths of Oak Leaf Park without the aid of any digital devices—just their own two legs and the rush of the wind.

"Last one to the duck pond buys ice cream!" Emma declares, her red curls bouncing as she hops onto her bike.

"Deal!" Nico agrees, eager to feel the real-life thrill that beats any video game high score. His heart races with friendly competition as they set off, pedaling furiously, laughter trailing behind them like a kite tail.

Piper watches from a distance, her green eyes sparkling with pride. She's perched at the top of the jungle gym, a lookout point for her brother's adventures. She sees the change in him; he's more present, more alive somehow, as if he's unlocked a new level in a game where the prize is pure joy.

"Go, Nico!" she cheers, knowing her words are carried away by the breeze but feeling like they matter all the same.

Lucas, who usually thrives on control, is different now, too. He's less about winning and more about the moment as he laughs alongside Nico and Emma. They're a team in this game of life, each bringing out a side of the others that was hidden before.

As they reach the duck pond, out of breath and grinning, Nico can't help but feel triumphant. Not because he won—they all arrive at the same time, collapsing in a fit of giggles—but because he's found a balance. The screen-time battles and controller-clutching seem distant now, replaced by real-world challenges and achievements.

"Guess we all owe each other ice cream," Lucas says, and they agree it's the best possible outcome.

Later, as the day wanes and shadows stretch across the playground, Nico returns home with Piper by his side. He slips into his routine of homework, a bit of gaming, and practicing his gymnastics moves—a handstand here, a triple back handspring there—with a newfound ease.

"Look at you, Mister Multitasker," Piper teases gently, watching her brother juggle his commitments like a pro.

"Hey, I learned from the best," he shoots back with a grin, acknowledging her influence.

The sun sets, casting a warm glow over the Carmichael household. Inside, the sound of Nico's laughter mingles with the gentle clicking of keys as he updates his YouTube channel—not just with gaming content now, but with snippets of his everyday adventures, too.

"Balance," Nico thinks, "is not just a gymnastics move. It's a way to play the game of life." He notices his dad in the backyard and throws on his hoodie to join him.

"Hey Dad, heads up!" Nico squints against the afternoon sun as he tosses a baseball.

His father stands a good distance away, glove ready, eyes twinkling with that challenge they always seem to hold whenever it's game time. He effortlessly catches the ball and throws it back.

"Come on, Nico! Keep your eye on the ball!" his dad calls out, voice warm and encouraging.

Nico nods, adjusting his stance. He stretches his arm back, fingers tightening around the seams of the ball, and with a swift motion, he throws. The ball cuts across the yard, a perfect spiral, and lands snug in his father's glove with a satisfying smack.

"Nice throw!" his father cheers, tossing the ball back.

The rhythm of catch feels natural, like the comforting tick of a clock. Back and forth, back and forth, each throw a little stronger, a little more confident. It's a simple joy, but it fills Nico with a sense of connection he hadn't realized he'd been missing during those long hours in front of the screen.

"Hey, Nico, ready to get creative?" Piper's cheerful voice interrupts their game.

"Sure, Piper," Nico replies, catching the ball one last time before jogging over to where his sister stands, her face alight with excitement.

Piper leads him into the house, to the dining table already strewn with construction paper, glue, and glitter. She holds up two paintbrushes like a magician flaunting wands. "Today, we're making a masterpiece," she declares, her green eyes dancing with anticipation.

"Let's do it," Nico says, heartened by her enthusiasm.

They settle into their chairs, and Nico feels the shift from physical exertion to creative expression. As they paint, Piper hums a tune he can't quite place, but it's catchy and he finds himself bobbing his head along rather than his typical reaction of being annoyed. They work side by side, sometimes silent, sometimes chatting about school, friends, and Piper's latest dance routine.

They get comfortable in their chairs, and Nico senses the change from physical activity to artistic creation. While they paint, Piper sings a song he doesn't recognize, but it's appealing and he ends up nodding his head with it instead of his usual response of irritation. They work next to each other, sometimes quiet, sometimes talking about school, friends, and Piper's newest dance move.

"Look, Nico, I'm mixing blue and yellow to make green!" Piper exclaims, her curls bouncing as she leans in to show him her discovery.

"Like your eyes," Nico comments, and Piper beams, proud of both her artwork and the comparison.

"Exactly!" she agrees.

Their paintings take shape, abstract and colorful, expressions of the moment. Nico's brushstrokes are bold and decisive, while Piper's dance across the paper with the grace of her namesake bird. They laugh at the splatters of paint that find their way onto their cheeks and foreheads.

"Artists at work," their mother jokes, peeking in to check on them.

"Or at play," Nico counters, realizing that this is just as much fun as any video game challenge.

As the light outside dims, they put the finishing touches on their creations. Piper's canvas is a whirlwind of color and movement, while Nico's is a constellation of shapes and patterns, orderly yet vibrant. Both siblings stand back, admiring their handiwork.

"Best day ever," Piper sighs contentedly, linking her arm with Nico's.

"Agreed," Nico says, and means it.

Together, they clean up the art supplies, leaving no trace of the mess behind, just like they always do after an epic gaming session. Only this time, the satisfaction comes not from virtual achievements, but from the real-life memories they've made.

"Tomorrow, let's go for a bike ride," Nico suggests, already looking forward to the next adventure.

"Okay! Race you to the park!" Piper challenges, and Nico grins, accepting the friendly competition.

"Game on," he replies, and they share a high-five, sealing the deal.

As they get ready for dinner, Nico glances back at their artwork drying on the table. This new game he's playing—the one with laughter, family, and fresh air—might just be his favorite yet.

CHAPTER 16
Puzzling the Coin

The basketball thuds against the blacktop as Nico dribbles with focus. He glances at his teammates, a grin spreading across his face. The sun is bright above them, casting long shadows of the fifth graders as they pass, shoot, and score under the clear blue sky.

"Nice shot!" he calls out to Emma, who just sunk a neat basket from the side of the court. Her ponytail swishes as she turns to high-five Lucas, their laughter mingling with the shouts and cheers of other kids enjoying recess.

Nico feels a rush of happiness. This—running around with friends, feeling his heart pound in his chest, the friendly competition—it's almost as thrilling as conquering a tough level on his favorite video game. Almost.

"Hey, wanna come over after school?" Nico asks during a brief timeout, wiping sweat from his brow with the back of his hand. "We can grab some snacks and hang out."

"Sounds awesome," Emma replies, her eyes lighting up. She's always up for an adventure, whether it's on a screen or in real life.

"Sure, let's do it!" Lucas chimes in, bouncing the basketball lightly on the ground. His energy is infectious, and Nico can't help but feel that today is going to be great.

"Alright, team huddle!" Nico says, pulling his friends close. "Let's play hard, play fair, and have fun. On three—"

"Team!" they shout together, hands stacked in the center before breaking apart and returning to the game.

The laughter and shouts rise high as the ball gets passed from one friend to another, each move building upon the last, creating a symphony of childhood joy. Nico steals the ball and makes a break for the hoop, the wind brushing through his messy blonde hair as he leaps and scores another two points.

"Yesss!" Nico pumps his fist in the air, and his friends rally around him, their shared excitement as palpable as the cool breeze whispering promises of more good times to come.

Nico's bedroom pulses with the energy of three friends. Sunlight dances through the window, casting playful shadows across the room as it watches over their after-school hangout.

"Hey Nico," Lucas starts, his voice cutting through the chatter like a knife through butter. "I've been meaning to ask, what happened to that magic controller?"

Nico pauses, a half-eaten chocolate chip cookie hovering just inches from his mouth. He hadn't thought about that old thing in ages, not since they'd all decided to spend more time outside, kicking balls rather than pushing buttons. "Yeah…" he replies cautiously, setting the cookie down on a napkin.

"Let's see it," Lucas says, leaning forward with that glint in his eye that usually means trouble.

"Ah, nah," Nico brushes off the request with a shake of his head, his short, messy blonde hair bouncing slightly. "It's way in the back of my closet." He gestures vaguely towards the mountain of board games, comic books, and assorted knick-knacks that have taken residence in the once orderly space. "I really don't want to get it out."

A beat of silence hangs in the air, thick with unspoken curiosity. Nico knows that controller is more than just a piece of plastic—it's a Pandora's Box of digital mystery. But right now, he's more interested in having fun with his friends.

"Come on, Nico," Emma's voice is gentle yet insistent, like the tug of a kite string on a breezy day. "It'll just take a second!" Her warm eyes are wide with that mix of curiosity and kindness that always seems to make things okay.

Lucas, on the other hand, is practically bouncing on the balls of his feet, his spiky hair looking like it might poke holes in the ceiling if he jumps any higher. "Yeah, what's the big deal?"

Nico sighs, feeling the resistance crumble like the edges of a well-loved comic book. He glances at his friends—one eager, the other earnest—and can't help but feel the tug of their excitement. "Okay, okay," he concedes with a resigned grin.

He kneels in front of his closet, where a fortress of clothes, shoes, games and action figures stand guard over the forgotten box. With careful hands, he begins to shift the chaos aside. Finally, his fingers brush against the lockbox tucked away, hidden like a secret base in a spy novel.

"Ah, here it is," Nico mutters, dragging the box out from its dusty cocoon.

With a flick, the lid pops open and Nico reaches in. But as he pulls the controller out, something unexpected happens. A small, round object tumbles from the confines of the box and clinks against the wooden floor.

"Hey, what's that?" Emma leans forward, her red curls bouncing as she peers at the shiny object now winking up at them from the carpet.

Nico's brow furrows as he sets down the controller. It's a coin—the kind you don't see in arcade machines or piggy banks—a glint of gold amidst the ordinary. How did that get there? His heart thumps a curious beat, echoing questions in his chest.

The coin lies there, as mysterious as the controller itself, a new enigma wrapped in an aura of digital legend. For a moment, they all just stare, caught up in the wonder of an unsolved puzzle.

Nico picks up the coin, rolling it between his thumb and index finger. It feels heavy, important somehow. The light catches on its surface, sending little reflections dancing across the walls of Nico's room.

"Probably one of Piper's pranks," he says with a nervous chuckle, shaking his head at the thought of his little sister's antics. He knows Piper loves to stir things up, her green eyes always twinkling with mischief.

"She's always messing with my stuff." It wouldn't be the first time she'd snuck something unexpected into his belongings to spark his curiosity.

"Can I see?" Emma asks, reaching out eagerly. Nico hands her the coin, and her fingers close around it like she's holding a piece of treasure.

"Whoa, it's heavier than it looks," she comments, passing it to Lucas, who also examines the coin with interest. Her brow wrinkles in concentration as he turns it over, inspecting both sides before nodding and giving it back to Nico.

"Okay, let's put it back now," Nico decides, more intrigued by the mystery of the controller's origins than the coin. The whole point was to show off the controller, not get sidetracked by what's probably just another of Piper's random trinkets.

Together, they carefully examine the controller, turning it over in their hands, feeling the familiar buttons. It's just an ordinary game controller on the outside, but they all know it holds secrets within.

"Time to pack it up," Nico says after a while, sensing that the magical moment has passed. They're here for good times, not to get lost in another adventure with this controller—yet. He places the controller back into the box along with the gold coin, and slides the lid shut with a soft thud.

"By the way, Nico, did you ever find out how the controller got those powers?" Emma asks, the question hanging in the air like the last leaf on a tree, stubborn and insistent.

Nico's fingers fidget with the hem of his T-shirt, his mind racing through every gaming session, every level conquered with the help of the mysterious controller. "Nope," he admits, his voice just above a whisper, so soft it almost blends into the hum of his computer.

Breaking the wonder in the air and realizes how late it has gotten Emma finally says, "I have to get home." Lucas follows her lead, the coin and its unanswered questions left behind as they head towards the door.

Nico waves goodbye as the door clicks shut. Now, it's just him, his room, and the aftermath of an afternoon well-spent. He straightens up, hands on his hips, surveying the territory of his bedroom kingdom. Plushies go back on shelves, comics stack neatly on the desk, and every stray sock finds its mate. He places the new controller on his desk while the old controller remains tucked away—its mysteries can wait for another day. As he works, his room transforms from a chaotic battlefield of fun into a tidy haven once more.

A sense of accomplishment blooms inside Nico. He's done this all on his own, without Mom's gentle nudges or Dad's playful chiding. It feels good—like leveling up in real life. He steps back, admiring the order he's restored, his heart lighter than it's been all day.

"Who knew cleaning could be so epic?" he chuckles to himself with a sense of triumph.

The room around him holds the memories of countless gaming marathons, but also the echoes of today's real-world adventures. It's a balance, Nico finally realizes. Screen time and sunshine, digital quests and driveway hoops—they all have their place in the life of Nico Carmichael, fifth- grade adventurer.

With his room now in order, Nico nods approvingly at his handiwork. It's more than just a clean space; it's a testament to his growing independence and his ability to juggle the worlds he loves—with a foot firmly planted in each one.

"Mission accomplished," he whispers, a grin spreading across his face. Now, he's ready to join his family for dinner, his appetite for life as hearty as ever.

Nico stands in the center of his room, a commander surveying his territory. He's just about to declare victory over the day when a strange sound pierces the silence.

Ting-a-ling-a-ling.

The noise comes from the direction of his closet, a soft but unmistakable jingle of coins. Nico freezes, his eyes wide behind his blank expression. "That's weird. What was that?" he whispers to himself, a shiver running down his spine. His heart beats a little faster, the thrill of the unknown mingling with a tinge of fear.

"Probably all in my head," he mutters, trying to shake off the eerie feeling. But the sound lingers in the air.

Nico lets out a nervous giggle, shaking his head as if to clear it of cobwebs and digital phantoms. With a shrug, he turns away from the closet. "Yikes, I gotta get out and touch more grass," he says, half-joking.

He reaches for the doorknob, giving his room one last approving glance. Then, with a click, he shuts the door behind him, leaving the mystery of the jingling coin behind—for now.

Bounding down the stairs, Nico's thoughts shift from his closet conundrum to the savory scents wafting from the kitchen. It's taco night, and he can already taste the spicy ground beef and tangy salsa. His stomach growls in anticipation, and he grins at the thought of sharing stories about his day with his family gathered around the dinner table.

"Hey, champ! Wash your hands. Dinner's almost ready!" calls Mr. Carmichael, his voice carrying from the dining area.

"Be there in a sec, Dad!" Nico replies, his voice bright with the promise of good food and even better company.

As he joins his family, Nico can't help but wonder about the coin he swears he saw – and heard, in his room. Yet, the plate of fried chicken on the dinner table quickly distracts him enough to leave the wondering for another day *in real life.*

Made in the USA
Columbia, SC
30 April 2024

0b6b92a9-13a3-4b49-92d5-2ea3683f2359R01